Art IS THE LIE
A VANDERBIE NOVEL

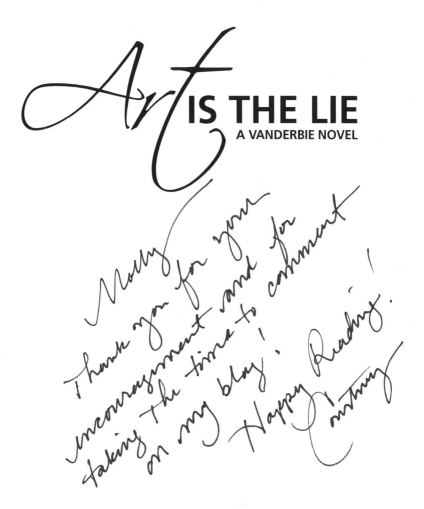

Molly
Thank you for your
encouragement and for
taking the time to comment
on my blog! Happy Reading.
Courtney

COURTNEY COOK HOPP

This book is a work of fiction. Any references to historical events, real people, or real locales are used fictitiously. Other names, characters, places, and incidents are the product of the author's imagination, and any resemblance to actual events or locales or persons, living or dead, is entirely coincidental.

ISBN: 978-1-4993-12331

The text type was set in Adobe Garamond Pro
Book cover and layout by Flair for Design
Author photo by Katy Tuttle Photography

Dedicated to my own
"Two Women Running on the Beach"
Carrie Cook Minns and
In Memory of Betty Jane Rice Cook

Art
is the lie
that enables
us to realize
the truth.

— *Pablo Picasso*

PROLOGUE

It would strike without warning — hard, splintering, non-breathable grief.

Like a hammer slammed down, its cruelty would pierce through every fiber of my body, leaving nothing but a fog of gray. Two and a half years of mind numbing gray.

But they lied.

About time.

About the healing power of time.

Because grief knocked me to the ground whenever it damn well pleased.

CHAPTER
1

The hammer's fluid arc swung forty-eight feet above my head, the black steel cutting through ribbons of purple and pink, woeven in the twilight sky. Up, down, up, down, the sculpture's endless rhythm predictable, keeping time to some unknown beat.

"CeeCee, come on," Grace shouted from the entrance of the Seattle Art Museum as a late summer breeze rolled up from the Puget Sound, swirling the salt air around me.

I tore my eyes from the Hammering Man sculpture, and followed Grace through the front doors of the SAM — away from my gray reality and into a vibrant world of dreamers.

"CeeCee, your aunt does not mess around," she shot over her shoulder. "She must donate loads of Franklins to get this kind of treatment."

"Doubtful," I replied, absorbing the art, the sophistication, the people — their collective donating power having lured them out for a private viewing of Picasso's work. I pushed my mess of long, strawberry blonde kinks behind my ear, realizing I should have tried harder to tame their out-of-control nature. "I'm fairly certain Uncle Russell's landscape business doesn't rake in this kind of cash."

Truth be told, I had no idea how Aunt Lucy scored the tickets, or why she would offer them to me. Had it been anyone else I'd have assumed it was a sympathy move, but that wasn't her style.

Instead, she planned and detailed the entire evening, quietly setting it into motion. The tickets, the town car, even enlisting Grace's mom to cover our island jailbreak with a "sleepover" fabrication, which helped to pull the wool over Dad's eyes. Not that it was hard to do. Not since the accident had left him blind.

"You'd be surprised the amount of money people pay out to avoid getting their hands dirty," Grace quipped, the spring of her black coils dancing around a brightly colored scarf.

"And you're suddenly an expert on the current pay structures of the working force?"

"Not me, girlfriend, but my parents pay a lot of people a lot of money to avoid doing a lot of things."

"Must be nice."

The distasteful smell of the toilet I scrubbed this morning still clung to the hair in my nose. Nobody came

to our house, ever, Dad muttering, *"If I can't see them, then I don't want them roaming around like ghosts."* Which was laughable, because he was the only ghost that slipped from room to room.

Grace pressed on with her superior rhetoric, the wake of our presence going unnoticed as we started up the stairs. "I figure it's my parents' way of making up for life times of past inequities."

"Maybe so," I said, unfazed by her usual bravado, her convictions, her hold-nothing-back attitude. She'd been that way from the day we met.

I'd been determined to hate everything about Vashon Island, Washington. That was until Grace waltzed in on my first day of art class two years ago, dropped down next to me, and began to ooze her infectious personality. It was refreshing, palpable. No hidden agenda or history to explain, just acceptance, allowing me to fly under the radar of her loud disposition.

Flight after flight, we continued up the stairs, aiming for the Special Exhibition Gallery on the top floor.

"This way," Grace pointed as we crested the last step.

I nodded, my boots striking against the marble floor, bouncing echoes off the static of quiet chatter as we crossed the threshold together — speechless.

Picasso.

Here.

Before me.

My breath caught as I drank in the palettes of brilliant color. To study his art in a book was one thing, but to see it up close — almost touch it, breathe in its scent — was like being in the room with Picasso as he was painting. Creating. Forging.

"Knock me out," Grace whispered over my shoulder.

I had no words, no reply as I released the trapped air from my lungs, the flow stirring an ache of another life. An ache that hung heavily on my shoulders.

My feet were unhurried as I crept from piece to piece, everything but the art fading from existence. I drank in the color, the boldness, the distortion camouflaging the stories hidden between the lines.

A wash of blue caught my eye, and I braced myself, my feet faltering as I neared the one in the corner.

The piece that held my mom — her story, her spirit — flush against the bright blues and explosion of disjointed energy.

My teeth sunk painfully into my lower lip, trying to override the mounting wave of grief inside me. I stared at the canvas of familiar women, their never-ending race having played out above my mom's desk. The outer rooms of the art gallery she owned in San Francisco had been filled with original creations, but centered directly above her office desk was a print of Picasso's "Two Women Running on the Beach" — a bond of sisterhood woven with the determination for victory.

The air thinned and I worked to gulp down a breath. And another. The women a painful reminder of the bond I was supposed to share with her. One that was stolen and wrapped tightly in twisted metal, broken. Forever.

I inched closer to the small canvas as I curled my arms tight around my chest. It was only a foot tall and a foot and a half wide, but the warmth exuded beyond its small borders, inviting you in, the women's laughter mocking the hush of the museum. I couldn't breathe. My body was seized by familiar, cruel pain threatening to split me in two, forcing a lone tear to trail down my cheek. I wanted to dive in, to run freely with the women, unburdened, without thought or care.

"It's a lie."

I jumped, the male voice displacing my pain, sending it scurrying back to its hiding place. I swiped my cheek dry and turned to face the intruder.

A guy about my age stood directly behind me. His dark hair a little too long, a little too messy, not quite covering a scar that ran from his left temple to the edge of his jawbone. Annoyed, I said, "Excuse me?"

Something almost imperceptible slid across his eyes as he looked into mine before his rough voice repeated, "It's a lie," and nodded toward my painting, causing the museum lanyard that dangled from his neck to swing back and forth.

I glanced around for Grace, but she was on the far side of the room, oblivious of the art critic in front of

me. I looked back at the stranger. His mossy green eyes rimmed with tired, dark circles, sunk deep on a bed of Mediterranean skin, drawing focus to the gentle slope of his nose.

I turned back to the painting before bitterly replying, "Of course it's a lie. Who would want to paint the ugly truth?"

He stepped to my side and stared.

I stole a glance. Our eyes tangoed briefly before I faced my running women again. "Has anyone ever mentioned that staring is rude?" I asked in hopes of jarring him along.

"It's only considered rude if you don't have a reason to stare."

I squared my shoulders, determined not to be undone by him. "And what possible reason could there be?"

"First, you're not the typical pre-viewing patron," he said matter-of-factly, while his pensive pools of murky green searched for something in mine.

I crossed my arms over my chest. "You mean I'm not old and rich?"

"Pretty much."

"Are you old and rich?" I asked, eyeing his disheveled appearance.

"No, but I work here, so I'm required to be in attendance."

"And?"

"And, what?"

"You said, 'First,' so I assume there's a 'Second.'"

"Second, not many people realize that art is a lie." His stare was disconcerting. "What made you say that?"

Mom's face flashed behind my eyes. "Gut. Life. Tragedy. Truth. Any or all of the above."

"Who are you?" The three words were a breath, bringing him a half a step closer, causing the temperature in the room to rise.

"No, I think the question is," I looked down at his name badge as I unbuttoned my coat, hoping for a small breeze, "Who are you, Quentin Stone? And what possible reason do you have for bothering me?"

"I thought you might have a question," he said, pointing back to my women. "You've been frozen in front of that painting for nearly twenty minutes."

Irritated, I looped my hair behind my ears. "So this is how you help patrons, by informing them that art is a lie before they can formulate their own opinion? I didn't realize there was a viewing time limit."

I tried to step around him and move to the next painting, but he shifted forward at the same time, causing an awkward, tripping, almost-hit-the-ground moment. His hand shot out and grabbed hold of my elbow. The warmth of the contact set off a strange tingling sensation at the base of my overly heated neck.

Still holding my arm, he asked, "Are you always this feisty, um, I didn't catch your name."

"That's because I didn't offer it. And what are you talk-

ing about, 'feisty'?" I ripped my elbow from his grip as a drop of sweat slid down my spine. The tingling sensation began to move. It crawled up my neck and across the top of my head, sharpening, like a thousand tiny needles penetrating my scalp. His dark emeralds, flecked with the slightest hints of gold, never strayed from my face as the walls of the cavernous exhibit hall began to push in claustrophobically. "Aren't you supposed to be helping patrons, rather than hindering them?"

"Yes, he is," a female voice said from behind us.

We both whipped around toward the new voice. I blinked, unsure if the pain searing through my mind was affecting my eyesight. I squeezed my eyes shut and wiped the sweat from my brow, trying to calm the storm brewing inside me.

But she was still there when I opened them. Elegant, in her daring eyelet dress and heels. Her gray, curly hair, which was barely harnessed to submission, was no match to the stance of her confident posture.

"We were talking about the truths found in Picasso's paintings," Quentin offered, nonplussed by the interruption.

"What . . ." My hand clamped over my forehead in an attempt to hold my shattering head together. It was a flash. A memory. A conversation I wasn't supposed to have heard.

"Did you tell her? You swore you wouldn't tell her," Dad had asked Aunt Lucy accusingly.

"She knows about Gretta, but not about your . . ."

Interrupting his sister, he spit out, "I don't want her help. I don't need her help."

"Peter, give Mother a chance. She wants to help."

"NO! I want nothing to do with that eccentric woman!" he'd bellowed, his blind eyes locking onto nothing, his harsh tongue a foreign language I didn't recognize.

Quentin Stone was staring at me. At the woman. The woman I'd seen before in framed photos at my aunt's house, but had never met. I dropped my hand from my head, my heart tripping over each resounding pound.

"Quentin, will you please introduce me to your friend?" she asked.

What? She knows random scar-face-art-museum-worker, but not me? Could she not know who I am?

"Um . . ." Quentin stammered. "Evelyn Vanderbie, this is, um . . ."

His hand brushed over my shoulder as my grandmother stretched hers out before me, waiting. I forced my hand out, the vibrations in my head bending painfully into a debilitating migraine.

"Um, sorry," Quentin said. "And your name is?"

"CeeCee," I heard my grandmother say as she clasped her fingers around my own.

A roar of blood whooshed behind my ears, forcing me to close my eyes as a barrage of color exploded behind them. Hues beyond anything I'd ever seen, vivid and

bright, boldly butting against one another before twisting into patterns more beautiful than the last. I wanted to disappear into myself, into the splendor, but my grandmother held tight to my hand. Squeezing. Grounding me to reality.

"C e e C e e . . ."

My name blew in like a whisper, scattering the vibrant colors and unleashing a horrific array of black and white images. One after another they painfully tumbled from the dark. Children screaming. Fires roaring. People drowning. Bodies teetering on the brink. Arms stretched out beyond the frames of images, begging to be understood.

I gulped for air, unable to grasp what was happening. I wanted the colors back, but the darkness prevailed, tipping me left. Right.

Skewing me into a backward slide.

My free hand struggled to grab hold of something solid as a final blast of white light washed everything out.

And then — nothing.

Black.

Everything went black.

CHAPTER
2

"CeeCee! Cee! Oh my god." Grace was yelling too close to my ear. "Cee, you have to wake up."

"Should I call an ambulance?" a male voice asked.

"I don't think that will be necessary." Another voice, a woman's voice.

My body was spent, drained of the beauty, the horror, feeling as if I'd run a marathon without ever having moved my feet. I lifted my heavy hand and pinched the bridge of my nose. It all came back — the dress, the unruly hair, the handshake — my grandmother.

"You see?" I heard her say. "Let's give her a moment. I'm sure she'll be just fine."

"What kind of cracker-jack wisdom are you spouting, lady?" Grace snidely asked.

Grace. Thank god for Grace.

Because I had no idea what just happened or if I was fine as the haunting images faded into the fuzzy gray of my mind.

"And you. You can take your hands off her," Grace said as she pulled me from the warmth I'd been cocooned in, my back shifting to the cold, hard floor. "CeeCee, you need to open your eyes."

"Please, Grace. Stop shouting." I forced my eyes open. Grace's face hovered over mine, her hair creating a strange, spongy halo effect. I turned my head to the body kneeling on the other side of me and caught sight of Quentin's brows knit harshly over his pensive eyes.

Grace probed on, touching her fingers to my cheek. "You're so pale. Are you okay? Can you get to your feet?" I did a quick mental checklist of my body, trying to figure out how and why it betrayed me.

"I'm fine." It didn't sound convincing, not even to my ears. "What…happened?"

"I think you fainted."

Fainted? I groaned but couldn't be sure if it had been audible or not.

"Is something hurt?" Quentin asked, his tone challenging, causing heat to flush my cheeks.

"No. Nothing's hurt." Except my ego. I needed out, the overwhelming urge of flight kicking in, because I had no explanation for what just happened.

"Maybe we should call your aunt," Grace said as I tried to stand. Quentin reached out to steady my rise,

but I leaned into Grace, not wanting to have what just happened, happen again. His hands retreated deep into his pockets as a rigid mask rolled over his face.

"No, really, I'm fine." I smoothed out the front of my shirt and pushed my unruly hair behind my ears, ignoring the tension radiating off of Quentin. The other gawkers in the room dispersed, pretending to go back to their own conversations.

"Delightful," my grandmother chirped, oblivious of the awkwardness. She turned her head slightly to a clean-cut gentleman I hadn't noticed hovering behind her. "Felix, isn't this delightful?"

He took a half of step forward, and quietly replied, "Yes, ma'am."

Her face looked amused by the whole episode, causing my spine to bristle. Maybe if I walked backward, down the stairs and out the front doors, I could start this night again. Stare up at the hammering man two minutes longer before entering, take the elevator instead of the stairs, not gaze at my running women for so long. I glanced over at the wall. They were still there, laughing and ridiculing our group that had congregated in front of them.

Grace looped her arm through mine, eyeing Evelyn suspiciously. "Thanks for your help, um . . .?"

"Evelyn," she replied, holding out her hand to Grace. I was tempted to slap it away, but was curious to see if Grace would hit the ground like I had.

Grace shook her hand without incident before turning to Quentin. "And you are?"

"Just a guy who works here." His feet shifted, antsy to move away from our random little entourage. His eyes darted to me before quickly looking away. "Who, needs to return to work."

"Thank you for your help, Quentin," my grandmother said with an expression I couldn't read. "It will always be appreciated."

He raised an eyebrow to her before purposely moving toward the exit without another wrod. I'd run too.

"Well, um . . ." I had no idea what to call the woman in front of me.

"CeeCee," Evelyn said, handing me a business card that Felix had procured from his folder. "I enjoy coffee, do you?"

"I guess," I said hesitantly.

"Then that's where we'll start. When you're ready, of course." Abruptly, without another word, she turned on her heels and walked away with Felix trailing behind.

I stared in disbelief. That's it? My eyes shifted to Grace and then back to the receding figure. I meet my long lost grandmother for the first time and all I get is a business card and an "I can't be bothered, so you call me" offer for coffee. I looked down at the elegant font that scrawled her name across the business card, disbelief icing over my heart. She could wait an eternity for the phone to ring.

"Who the hell was that?" Grace asked as she pulled me toward the door.

I was pliable putty, unable to fight Grace's pull to the exit. Picasso's beauty faded as we rounded the corner out of the room. I drew in a deep breath. And another.

"Evelyn, of course." I couldn't bring myself to mention she was the Grandmother I'd never met, who obviously could care less about my existence. That would be too humiliating to confess. Even to Grace.

"Do you know Evelyn?"

"No. I don't know the first thing about her." Which was the truth. I knew nothing about that woman.

Grace stopped and looked me in the eye. "Cee, are you okay? Do you want to sit or something?"

"No," I sighed. I didn't want to sit and linger, wondering if Evelyn would appear again. Or Quentin. "I need air. Fresh air. I need to get out of this building."

We pushed our way out the front doors, the late summer evening still holding the chill of fall at bay. I looked up, just as the Hammering Man's hammer descended down above us, threatening to knock us both to the ground.

"What happened in there?"

"I have no idea." I tore my eyes from the hammer, needing to clear the muddled chaos that still trickled through my head. "You saw more than I did."

"All I saw was a bunch of commotion, and you, out cold, chillaxin' on some hottie's lap with his arms wrapped around you."

"Seriously?" Embarrassment crept up my cheeks. "I was in his lap?"

"Yeah," she snorted. "I'm surprised he didn't set off your anti-guy repellant."

"I'm not 'anti-guy.'"

"Girl, you are about as warm and fuzzy as a porcupine when it comes to the advancements of the opposite sex," she said, trying to stifle her laughter. "But, mm-mmm, you do know how to land. If you're going to pass out, make sure you drop on top of a rugged, delicious morsel. Did you check. Him. Out?"

"Trust me, he wasn't all that delicious," I replied, even though I couldn't quite shake the tantalizing green eyes from my mind. "Besides, I thought you liked your boy toys honed and polished."

"For that bad boy, I'd make an exception."

"Bad boy?" I asked with a raised eyebrow.

"Boys who tow the line don't end up with scars running down their face. If it had been me nestled in his arms," she said, waggling her finger in the air, "I wouldn't have been in any hurry to giddy-up."

"Correct me if I'm wrong, but weren't you the one who pulled me off his lap?"

"Oh, yeah," she said, unable to hold back her laughter any longer, her hair dancing with her glee. "A jealous fit must of taken hold."

"Obviously."

Minutes proceeded like hours as we made our way back to Grace's house. I was convinced I would never sleep as I lay in the dark listening to her slow, even breathing, my brain stuck on replay. Over and over the images of the night trampled through my mind. The painting. The scar. The colors. The horror. Evelyn. No hugs, no emotional reunion, only coffee and a hand shake.

Time ticked. Tocked. Taunting. Holding sleep hostage. My mind trapped in an endless spin cycle. Until, finally, the wee hours pulled me down into a strange and restless state of unconsciousness.

My women danced across their canvas, escaped their boundaries, and gracefully floated through the air, down to a murky bed of green.

It was peaceful.

Quiet.

Fluttering like a parachute. Spinning. Bending. Morphing. Forming eyes. Eyes that stared into my own, reaching out and drawing me in. With arms and a body. His scar glimmering in the pool of silver light that shimmered down from above. We twirled to silence. Dipped into nothing. Only the cool air whispered fluffy, cotton flakes across our skin.

I leaned into his protective arms as the sky began to burn red. Heat sweltered up around us before a curtain blissfully fell black over the rain of fiery debris plummeting down.

22

CHAPTER

3

It was chaos, beyond chaos, as I maneuvered my mom's old ragtop Karmann Ghia through the school parking lot. And it was pouring down rain, a fine tribute to mark the first day of my senior year.

Two weeks had slid by.

Exactly.

Fourteen days since I'd forced the awful black and white images into the deep files of my mind. Fourteen days of pretending I hadn't come face to face with a grandmother I'd never met. Fourteen days before Grace finally quit asking me if I was okay, or if I felt faint.

There was nothing to touch. Nothing tangible that screamed out the events of that night. Only a business card propped up on my dresser, which I worked hard to ignore. I hadn't heard from my grandmother or both-

ered to call her, my pissed-off-ness with her indifference always coming between any two rational thoughts my brain tried to produce.

And him. Embarrassment kept my mind from wandering over his existence.

I dashed across the parking lot, the downpour reenacting my morning shower and undoing my efforts to tame the kinky mess on top of my head. I moved through the school and pulled a damp piece of paper from my pocket, attempting to read the locker number and break-in code bleeding into the fibers of the paper. I found my small slice of metal stamped with the appropriate number and fumbled with the dial.

"Vanderbie! Hey, Vanderbie!"

I looked up. Sean. The only other personality able to rival the force of Grace's at Vashon High. He strutted — he always strutted — sporting the usual student garb of jeans and a form fitting t-shirt, both looking amazingly dry.

"Hey, Sean." I focused my attention back on the dial, determined to make my second attempt work. "How did you escape the pre-school drenching?"

"Skill," he answered with a smirk.

I tried to lift the handle. No go. "Damn," I muttered with a kick to the door.

"It's not Fort Knox, Vanderbie. Three numbers, three turns, and voilà."

"Did I mention breaking and entering aren't part of

my future calling?" I quipped back, making a third attempt.

"Give me that." He snatched the piece of paper from my hand and stepped between the locker and me. An overwhelming cloud of cologne descended down, forcing me to step back as he manipulated the dial. The smug look was back in his round eyes, peeking out from behind his jet-black hair as he pulled the locker open. "Like I said, 'voilà'."

"Now I know who to call for my next big heist." I threw my wet jacket into the locker and kicked the door closed.

"For you Vanderbie, anytime." And there it was, his wicked, heart-melting smile that could make a statue lift the corners of its lips. I couldn't stop my own grin from making an appearance.

Sean looked down and caught sight of my upturned lips. "You really have a great smile, Vanderbie, smooths out your sharp edges. You should use it more often."

His voice was quiet, friendly, reminding me of my brother Foster. Flustered, I pulled the strap of my messenger bag over my head and muttered, "What are you talking about? I smile."

He leaned in as if imparting a deep secret. "Not often, Vanderbie. Not often."

Everything buzzed like white noise, holding me hostage to his words that pulled on emotions better left alone. His cologne swirled around us, and I wiggled my

nose to try and keep from sneezing, but the fumes won the battle of the airwaves. The odd moment dispelled.

"Aa-chu," I blew and rubbed my nose. "Dude, did you pour an entire bottle of pretty water on yourself this morning?"

"Oh, you know you love it," he said, his wicked smile back. "Or are you afraid you might, you know . . . pass out."

My body relaxed, happy to be on safe conversation ground, even if it was at my expense. "Yeah, well, this girl would prefer a little more o'natural stink to that pungent cloud of musk you bathed in." We stepped out from the lockers and moved into the flowing stream of students heading to class. Sean was a flirt through and through with every girl, somehow making you feel recognized and not demoralized.

"How's your old man?"

"Nothing's changed," I answered curtly, pretending to read my class schedule. Nothing and everything.

"Ah." He waved to someone I didn't know, blissfully changing the subject. "Who've you got for homeroom?"

Letting out a sigh, I answered, "History with hard-nose Sherrell. Someone in administration has it out for me."

"Nah, he's not too bad."

"This coming from the collegiate football player already on track to a full-ride scholarship."

Grinning, he threw his arms out wide and said, "What can I say? I've got a gift—I'm adorable and happen to be able to throw a football."

"Hence the cavalier attitude toward any threat to your GPA. We should all be so lucky to be born with a gift." I was only kind-of teasing. Sean managed pretty decent grades even though his picture could be found next to the definition for jock. But it was his easy-going banter that I safely sunk into, avoiding any type of deep conversation.

"Hey! Sean. CeeCee," Grace's voice called out.

We both did a simultaneous scan and spotted Grace's hand bobbing up and down over the heads of the other students. We pushed our way over and found Dylan and Avery relaxing on a bench next to her.

"Glad to see you've all gathered to give me my proper glory," Sean said as we approached.

"Just call us your glory puppets," Grace retorted, her eyes shining more than her voice. I looked between the two of them, wondering if there was something going on.

There never used to be, back when Grace had foisted me upon her posse of friends. They really didn't have a choice — about me, or her for that matter. She'd moved to Vashon the year before me and decided Sean, Dylan, and Avery, who were island lifers, would be the perfect blend for her to hang with. She didn't ask, she just decided. The same way she'd decided they would accept me, no questions asked.

Avery's long, dark hair swung over her face as she nodded in Grace's direction. "Sean, you do remember who you're competing with for attention, right?" Her eyes smiled their friendly gleam as she winked at me, never a hint of pity displayed for the girl who was down one parent, and out an emotional connection to the other.

Without so much as a missed beat, Grace countered, "Listen, sister, I don't need to compete for attention. It just naturally comes my way."

"Yeah, like Vanderbie naturally passes out," Dylan joked, stretching over to Sean for a fist bump.

"You're hilarious, funny man," throwing my finger in Dylan's face. "You do not want to mess with me."

He unfolded his lanky frame and stood, towering over me. "Oh, I'll mess with you, Vanderbie." The heat in his tone promised something I was not interested in.

I stepped back and put my hands in the air. "Hey, I just want to know how much longer I'm to be the butt of your jokes?" I asked, shooting Grace a slitty-eyed look.

Waving me off with a flick of her wrist, she said, "Girl-friend, you knew I wouldn't be able to keep that kind of thing to myself."

"Remind me not to tell you my deepest, darkest secrets."

"Now those, I can keep," she said with a smile that didn't quite convince me.

"Hey, Sean!" We all turned our heads to a group of sophomoric girls on the approach. "Good luck at the game on Friday."

"Thanks girls. I expect to see you cheering us on in the stands." Sean gave them one of his heart-melting grins and waved as they giggled by.

"Good luck at the game on Friday," Grace mimicked under her breath. "Could they be any more obvious?"

Sean turned back to us, ignoring Grace. "I expect you all to be there on Friday giving me my proper glory, too."

"Isn't it supposed to rain on Friday?" I asked, not the least bit excited about getting drenched while watching yet another sporting event.

"Oh, our poor little California girl," Grace teased, making her voice sound sad and pathetic. "Still not used to seasons actually changing."

"This coming from the girl raised in the heat of the south. Don't you melt in the rain?"

"You know it, but my people have spent lifetimes adapting."

"Of course they have."

The bell rang, sending us in five different directions.

The next four days were a repeat of Monday, with the exception that I knew where my classes were and by Wednesday, I'd managed to open my locker.

CHAPTER
4

My dad whispered up behind me like a ghost, stirring the silence in the house. "Where are you going?"

I sighed into the open front door, the words of Jane Eyre dangled in my clamped hand. Up until that moment, I hadn't decided where I was going. I needed out. Away from the throat closing stillness that always engulfed me on the weekends leaving me to crave Monday's return. Back to a routine that had nothing to do with the shell of my dad.

"Up to the art room to read." The half-hearted reply floated off my lips and caught in the breeze, the wind carrying it down the long gravel driveway. From under the rim of my cabbie hat, I stared, believing I could see the letters, the words, the formed sentence, drifting away.

Suddenly, the urge to float away with them tempted my feet to follow.

"Mmm."

The low rattle of his tone pulled my eyes back in the house, but he had already shuffled away. Another drop of loss fell inside me, sizzling on flames of nothingness.

I stepped out onto the front porch and yanked the door closed harder than I needed to, setting the porch swing into motion. I'd intended to veer left to my small art room above the detached garage, but my feet crunched on the sharp bits of gravel and picked up speed, propelling me down the driveway and off the property.

Home was no longer home. Not since the accident. Not since Mom died and Aunt Lucy had convinced Dad to move us north to this desolate island, a stone's throw from Seattle. The conversations, the attempts at niceties, the mundane motions of life, they were thin like a shadow, casting a gray hue over each day, slowly painting over the memory of my mom.

Her face. Her gestures. Her voice.

I struggled to hear her voice. The soft velvet tones that would pour out and wrap around me. Embrace me. Encourage me.

My walk was aimless. One street turned into the next, eventually spitting me out in the throbbing metropolis of Vashon Island — a two-way main street with exactly one blinking red light. I followed the sidewalk south, moving

in and out of the long shadows cast down by the indecisive tumbleweed of clouds.

Small town hellos reached out to greet me with soft smiles, their forms shimmering in the storefront windows. They flowed from glass to glass, until one bent into something familiar, distorting like a house of mirrors. Blood roared through my veins, freeing goose bumps to speckle down my arms as I spun around. My eyes darted from one person to the next, trying to register what I thought I had seen but couldn't define. But there was nothing. Nothing physical. Only a déjà vu that boiled inside me, churning up a kernel of unease. I continued to move, my heart keeping time with my new quickened pace.

I jaywalked across Main Street with a last look over my shoulder, chiding myself and the bristly hair on the back of my neck. This was Vashon Island after all, not some crime infested inner city. Unsure of where to go, I slipped into a dimly-lit restaurant. A non-ringing bell "danked" against the door, announcing my arrival.

"Sit wherever you want," the guy behind the register called out. He didn't bother to lift his eyes from whatever he was reading.

The door closed behind me, sealing my decision to stay in the faint smells of fried food and sanitizer.

The diner was nearly empty, except for an overly affectionate couple near the front. With one last glance out

the window, I moved deeper into the restaurant and sat at a table near the back, hoping to rein in my delusional thoughts.

The guy from behind the counter ventured out and splashed down a glass of ice water and a menu. "Do you want something else to drink?" he asked, his rolled up sleeves exposing layers upon layers of colorful tattoos.

I looked down at my Jane Eyre book still in hand and back out the front window. I had no purse. No wallet. No cell phone to call Grace to come get me.

"Are you expecting someone?" he asked.

My head snapped back to him. "Um, no. No one else. I'll just have water."

Without a word, he turned and walked away.

I tapped nervously on the cover of my book, unsure of how I was going to execute a "dine and ditch." Or if I was ready to.

I slunk low in my seat and flipped the book open to the dog-eared page, pretending to read about Jane's miserable life at Lowood School. It could be worse, I reminded myself as my eyes skimmed the page, I could be Jane.

My not-so-friendly tattooed waiter reappeared, interrupting the massive typhus epidemic sweeping through Jane's school. He re-filled my water glass, managing to spray water everywhere with the forceful stream coming from the pitcher.

"Do you know what you want?"

I picked up the menu and pretended to look it over. "I haven't decided yet." The "dank" of the dead bell rang again, admitting someone else into this haven of congeniality.

Tattoo guy called out over his shoulder "sit wherever," blocking my view of the door. He looked back at me and asked, "Any decisions?"

"No," I said, setting the menu on the table.

He rolled his eyes and stepped away from the table. Directly behind him were the tantalizing green eyes from my dream. The very ones I pretended didn't exist.

"Quentin," my strangled voice rang in disbelief.

His surprise mirrored my own, but quickly dissolved into expressionless lines that rippled an uneasy quiver through my stomach. He didn't budge. Only the subtle flinching of his jaw, shifting the line of his scar in and out of place, hinted that he wasn't a statue. It took my mind nano-seconds to recreate an image of me passed out on his lap, instantly shooting flames of heat up my cheeks.

"Um, hello?" I finally said, attempting to break his odd trance.

Nothing, until he muttered something I couldn't understand. The pause that lingered was brutal, heightening the clanking coming from the kitchen to an overwhelming stream of static.

"Excuse me?"

And still he didn't reply. He closed his eyes, as if in pain, murmuring almost inaudibly, ". . .worst luck . . . seriously, can't be here . . ."

Of course he didn't want to be here, with me, the strange girl who stares at half-naked Picasso paintings before passing out.

"Unfortunately, you are here," I said, stating the obvious, the flames on my cheeks moving deeper into my hairline. "You've landed on the island of peace, love, and happiness."

His eyebrows furrowed deep over his sunken emerald eyes, the tired black circles from the night of the Picasso show, all but gone. He remained silent, the odd moment turning stranger by the second. I broke the intense stare and pretended to look for my place in my book.

"What are you doing here?"

My head popped up at the sound of his full voice. "Um, I stepped in for . . ." Honestly, I had no idea what I was doing in here. My eyes darted to the window, unsure if the nonsense I had felt fifteen minutes ago still lingered outside. His head cocked slightly. "Um . . . I was thirsty?"

He eyed the glass of water on the table before returning his intense gaze back at me. "I meant the island. What are you doing on the island?"

His scrutiny was making me nervous. Not the freak-me-out nerves of whatever was outside, but the I-should-

have-combed-my-hair type of unfamiliar nerves. I began to ramble. "The story in its entirety is long and tedious, but if you skipped to the last page, you would discover I live here. Well, actually, 'live' might be too strong of a word. The house I reside in is on the island, but the hours I'm not sleeping are spent plotting my island escape." I reached for my water to stop the spew of words from my mouth. It was too much information. I knew it the minute he pushed his hand through the clean, tight waves of his dark hair.

I was about to refine the story when tattoo waiter came back and placed a second menu on the table. "Can I get you something to drink?" he asked, assuming Quentin was with me.

Quentin's eyes did a barely distinguishable scan of the room before he slid the strap of a camera bag he'd been holding off his shoulder. "A Coke."

I closed my book and sat up straight, my stomach a sudden mess of nerves. He was staying? Why was he staying?

"Jane Eyre — for school?" He nodded to the book as he sat down across from me. "Isn't she the one who falls for a guy hiding his deranged wife in the attic?"

I looked down at Jane's coquettish smile before my eyes found his again. "Doesn't everyone have a deranged someone whispering around their house?"

"Not currently."

"I believe that makes you the exception."

His eyes darkened. "Maybe. But if an island evacuation is what you're planning, doesn't that guarantee a fateful demise for the deranged person locked up at your house."

"Death cannot be stopped," I said harsher than I'd intended.

"But it can be buffered."

"No, actually, it can't," I challenged. "Death does not take hostages, only members." My words hung between us, the surreal conversation floating a cloud of confusion through me.

Tattoo guy walked up, and set down Quentin's Coke. "Are you guys eating?"

"No," we both spouted at the same time. He shook his head and walked away again.

I watched Quentin take a long sip of his Coke, his unhurried movement somehow settling, soothing over my ragged lines of tension. When he set his drink down, he asked, "How do you know Evelyn?"

Caught of guard by the question, I blurted, "I don't." I was in no way prepared to have a long-lost grandma discussion with a complete stranger.

"But she knew your name."

"Knowing someone's name doesn't mean you know them. I know your name is Quentin Stone, but I don't know the first thing about you."

"You know I'm not currently housing a deranged person. That's more than most people know."

I shifted and tucked a loose piece of hair back under my hat. "Lucky me."

"And I know you have a propensity for fainting while viewing Picasso."

"Hardly the fault of the paintings."

"Then what caused you to faint?"

I had yet to answer that question myself, so I asked, "How do you know Evelyn?"

"Everyone knows Evelyn."

I lifted an eyebrow. "Everyone?"

"She's a collector. I met her through my mom a long time ago, but she's also one of the top donors at the SAM, part of the President's Circle."

"Is that a big deal?"

"It is if you want a presence in the art world."

"Ah," I said, more confused than ever about Evelyn and why Dad wanted nothing to do with her. "And what exactly is your job at the SAM, aside from heaping opinions on unsuspecting viewers?"

"That is my job," he said arrogantly, "when I'm not shooting my own photos."

"Are you a student?" My face crinkled as I tried to picture him strutting around the University of Washington campus with a camera in hand.

"A student?" he said, mulling over my words. "Um, of photography. Today, I'm in search of long, creepy shadows."

"If it's long, creepy shadows you're wanting, you should go down to Point Robinson Lighthouse. The place is loaded with them," I said off-hand, offering my best tourist guide information in hopes he might take the bait and leave. "And, if you're lucky, you might catch a glimpse of the deranged woman they keep locked up at the top of the tower."

"Okay." He stood abruptly and pulled cash from his pocket, tossing it on the table. "You'll come, show me the shadows, and protect me in case the deranged lady plans a sneak attack."

His quick movements and what I think is an invitation, throw me off. "And why should I risk my life for yours?"

"Because you owe me." His tone was unwavering, persuasive, sending all common sense fleeing from my mind. Noting my hesitancy, he added, "I did, after all, keep you from cracking your head open at the SAM."

CHAPTER
5

My plan was to follow behind him, hide in his shadow, assess the passer-byers on the sidewalk before stepping out of the restaurant. But he waited, holding the door open for me, chivalry beating out my paranoid nerves.

My eyes adjusted to the bright light and found nothing. No one waiting or watching. The only abrupt movement was my overly active imagination.

The door swished closed behind us, and Quentin said, "Why don't we take my car."

"Um, sure," not mentioning I didn't have a car for us to take. I followed him down the street to an army green Range Rover, circa not much newer than my Karmann Ghia. He opened the passenger door and waited as I climbed inside the pristine interior.

My stomach made a series of somersaults at my rash decision to get in a car with a complete stranger. What the hell was I doing? Ignoring my intuition, I pointed him south on Vashon Island's two-lane highway after he asked which way to go.

I stole glances of him out of the corner of my eye as he quietly manipulated the car per my directions, but he offered no conversation in return. The silence should have been painful, choking, like at home, but it was different, soft in a way I couldn't quite place my finger on.

We rolled our way down Point Robinson Road to a parking lot that sat above the lighthouse. Glimpses of the tower peaked through the swaying treetops, the soft cawing of seagulls a reminder that water was near.

"The lighthouse is this way." I stepped out of the car and pointed to a narrow path that vanished into the woods.

He nodded and grabbed his camera case from the backseat.

We ventured down through the dense mini-forest, slow and deliberate. Quentin stopped often to take pictures, never rushing a shot or becoming distracted by my presence as the soft click of the shutter opened and closed to a private view intended only for his eyes. His concentration emanated a deep intensity from his face, etching hard lines across his cheeks. The harshness portrayed a red flag that should've had my nerves jumping and my

feet moving in the opposite direction, but instead, it left me curious.

"How long have you been interested in photography?" I asked as we broke free from the trees. The warmth of the sun embraced us and pushed away the damp chill of the woods.

"Awhile."

"Any other photographers in your family?"

He shook his head no while spying something else through his lens.

"How about brothers or sisters?"

He turned his head from the back of his camera to look at me. I could read the hesitation in his eyes. "One of each."

He stepped away — avoiding my eyes, my questions.

Moving across the clearing, he aimed for the backside of the lighthouse and called over his shoulder, "I'm going to head around to the far side of the tower."

I picked up my pace. "Is that my cue to follow and protect you from the crazy lady?" I asked jokingly. "I don't want to be accused of shirking my duties."

"Loyalty. A rare commodity." There was no humor in his tone. We walked past a wall of luscious green trees, lined like soldiers down to the waters edge. They stood strong, daring the water to try and take over any more land.

"Are they older or younger?"

"Who?"

"Your brother and sister."

"Older."

We came to the back of the non-working lighthouse, now owned by the parks department, and walked the length of the building protruding from the tower. "Where do they live?"

"Do you always ask this many questions?"

We rounded the corner of the building, the Seattle skyline visible to the north. "Do you always avoid questions?" I countered.

He stopped abruptly and spun around, his tall frame loomed over me. "San Francisco." The air pulsed with his dubious stare. "They both live in San Francisco."

My nerves reared up and my mouth began an uncensored spout of words. "I'm sure you were dying to ask, but I'll save you the breath. I have one brother." I lifted my hand to block the glare of the sun as I looked up at his unreadable face. "Foster. Older. He just left for his first year at Cal Poly San Luis Obispo."

He shook his head in bewilderment. "Who are you?"

"You used up that question the last time we met. You need to work on your repertoire."

Not waiting for a reply, I moved beyond him and focused in on the shoreline.

I froze.

It began.

Tingles. Painful tingles. Up the back of my neck. Rocking me to the core as they marched with purpose over the top of my head, puncturing every pore like the rhythm of a sewing machine's needle. The pain stealing the breath from my throat.

The colors returned with a burst, displacing the pain as they began their intoxicating dance, spinning and morphing into patterns of brilliance. My body swayed and my limbs softened in response.

"CeeCee?" Quentin's voice fluttered through the colors, and replaced them with a hail of dark images. One after the other, they fell heavily inside me.

Bam.

Bam. Bam!

A small rowboat thrashed in the water. Cracks of lightening flashed across the sky. Storm water rose everywhere, threatening to topple the little wooden boat.

"CeeCee, do you want to sit down?" His words were barely a whisper above the roaring silence in my head. Words I couldn't respond to, react to, my tongue latched down, every muscle in my body forced to focus on the horror unfolding before me.

I sucked in a deep breath not yet stolen from me, trying desperately to regain control of my slipping mind. But the images pressed on. Painfully. Demanding my full attention. Demanding I focus solely on the shadowy figure that had emerged in the chaos. A figure trapped in the boat, clinging desperately to the sides.

No longer able to stand under the pressure, the pain, my body dropped. A ring of warmth circled my waist, softening the fall.

"CeeCee?" His voice grounded me, a touchstone to reality, pacing my heart as the images raced by.

I drew my legs up and curled into myself, the dark storm sucking me in deeper and deeper, crossing over the threshold of reality. Water. Everywhere. Rising violently. I gasped for air, wanting to reach out, to rise above the chaos and grab hold of the shadowy silhouette clinging for life in the fragile boat.

And then it was gone, sucked through a vortex, leaving only a wash of gray.

My body sunk into warmth. Exhausted. The last of the piercing needles making a hasty retreat.

"CeeCee? Are you okay? Should I call someone?"

I held completely still as my insides quaked, unsure of what was happening to me. I sucked in a short breath and another, praying when I opened my eyes that the world would still be round, rotating on its even-keeled axis and that the boy with green eyes would vanish before he could confirmed what I wasn't willing to admit to myself. I was losing it.

"CeeCee. Say something. Two minutes ago you had no trouble forming words." His rough fingertips brushed my cheek as he pushed back erratic strands of hair that had escaped from under my hat. "You're face is so pale."

Unable to avoid the inevitable, I opened my eyes and turned to his face that was inches from my own, my back cradled against his propped up knee. My eyes latched on to his furrowed brows, and I allowed myself to swim in the soft pools of green that lay below them, safely avoiding the hazardous wasteland of my mind.

He blinked, bringing my trance to an end. I looked out across the dock. The endless planks hovered over the gray water, dropping off into nothing. An overwhelming urge to see what lay beyond welled up inside me.

"Is something wrong with you?" His tone was patronizing, effectively breaking the intimate moment. "Do you have these types of spells often?"

"No!" I blurted at the thought, getting my feet underneath me. I didn't want his condescending sympathy. "Never. Not once."

Quentin was quick to grab my arm. "Don't rush on my account."

I couldn't stop. I had to stand. I had to walk away from him. The end of the dock was calling out to me. My steps were small. Babyish. The boards creaking under my weight. I didn't know what I was looking for, I only knew I had to look. I had to see if anything was down there.

I inched closer, the images in my mind painting a picture before I saw it, before I leaned over the edge and found a small wooden rowboat listing gently on the calm waters. The same boat trapped in my head. My legs wobbled and goose-bumps broke out everywhere.

46

Quentin grabbed my shoulder and pulled me back. "What are you doing?"

Gently the boat rocked back and forth. Empty. "This can't be," I murmured. "How can this be the same boat?"

"The same boat as what?" He pulled me back a few more inches.

"The same boat . . ." I looked back at the spot where I'd been overcome by the images. I looked at Quentin's face, his eyes returning me to the SAM, to the flurry of images I'd seen that night, almost certain that one had been of this very dock and boat. "How is that possible?"

"How is what possible?"

Unable to stop myself, I said, "I've seen this boat before."

"You've been on this boat?"

I was trapped in a bubble of confusion. My words tried to piece together what my mind couldn't process. "No, I've never been on the boat, but I've seen it."

"CeeCee, you're not making any sense." His voice hardened in frustration. "When did you see it?"

"Um, right . . . right before I fainted at the SAM." There. It was out. Like a live wire loose in the air, poised to send people running from me. The truth that something besides fainting had happened. The truth of how normal I wasn't.

The lull that hung in the air was a familiar, tense and silent. Painful gears turned, assessments were being made — scales balanced.

"I don't understand a word you're saying," he said, running his hand through his hair. "You saw a piece of art that looked like this boat?"

I didn't understand what I was saying either, because what my mind hinted at wasn't possible. The fog inside me began to lift and an uneasy feeling descended down, stalling my verbal processing. "You're right," I said, latching on to the only plausible explanation. "I probably saw a piece of art at the SAM that reminded me of this boat."

He thrust an accusatory finger at the lifeless boat. "CeeCee, there are no works of art at the museum that look like this boat."

I pulled free from the spell the tiny boat had cast over me, too tired to understand, too embarrassed to try and explain. "Your photos. You should get the rest of your pictures before you lose the light."

I could see a debate slide across his eyes as he held mine. "The photos can happen another day. We should get you home." Abruptly, he turned and headed back to the car, the out of balance scale sending him rocketing from the island. Away from the crazy girl.

CHAPTER
6

My brush stroke was tense, the bristles bending awkwardly under the pressure of my fingers. I focused all of my energy on the hue of crusted amber, determined to keep my mind clear of the garbage it continued to regurgitate. I forced the brush down the canvas, my wrist bent just the way Mom had taught me. Hours she would spend with me, her patience endless, stroke after stroke.

I dropped my hand and stared at the line of color. It wasn't right. Nothing felt right. I threw my paintbrush onto the pallet of colors, leaving the floodgates of my mind open to be inundated with the images I'd tried to suppress. Quentin. The lighthouse. The boat. The shadowy figure clinging for life as the storm waters attempted to thwart their efforts.

Was it supposed to be me? Drowning?

I shoved my balled fists against my eyes, trying to rub out what lay behind them. Every free moment of the past couple of weeks I'd spent holed up in my art room. Hidden, as I waited and wondered, when and if my mind would turn on me again and make another painful strike, leaving me stripped of all rational explanation.

The sound of tires crunching on the gravel driveway announced a welcome distraction. I shuffled over to the dormer window, twisting my out of control hair up into a knot before shoving a paint brush through it. Grace and Avery stepped out of Grace's car and headed toward the house. I hesitated before rapping on the window, unsure if I had it in me to be social.

Acknowledging me with a wave, they altered their course to the stairs that led up the side of the garage.

They disappeared from view as my forehead came to rest on the cool glass. I closed my eyes and sucked in a deep breath, mentally preparing myself for Grace's intense level of social banter. As my lids fluttered open, a slow moving car passed the end of our gravel driveway, spiking a surge of adrenaline through my veins. An old green Land Rover, like Quentin's. It couldn't be.

I blinked. Shook my head. Looked again.

Nothing. It was gone.

I rubbed my tired eyes, unsure if I'd imagined it or not. Of course I did. I turned from the window, unwilling to fall victim to my mind's pranks.

Again.

I was becoming delusional. It was no different than the figure in the boat, or the images I saw the night at the SAM. Maybe I was the deranged lady that needed to be locked away.

The thump of feet on the stairs brought me back to reality. I shook off my misguided sight and returned to the canvas, trying to brush in some final details.

"Okay, Cee," Grace said as the door flung open and she and Avery stepped in. "Let's see it."

I squinted, brushing wisps of highlights to the dark hair on the canvas. "Hello to you, too."

"Hello is a formality we've moved way beyond," she chirped and gave the door a back-kick closed. "Although, with your recent MIA status, maybe formal greetings are back in order."

I knew it was true. I'd been in full avoidance mode, embarrassment of possibly fainting keeping me out of the public eye.

"And you look like crap," Grace commented, her eyes giving my disheveled appearance a once over.

"You can ignore her," Avery chimed in. "She's a bit bent by a stupid rumor floating around."

"It's not stupid."

"It is stupid," Avery retorted in her usual black and white tone.

"What's the rumor?" I looked up as they neared. They

ART IS THE LIE

both looked crisp against the fuzziness of my mind. Bold and put together, swimming through my world of gray.

"Sean's interest has been caught by a little, you know," Avery said as she leaned in and whispered, "T and A."

"Well, which is it?" Glad to have someone else's problems to focus on. "A 'T' or an 'A'?"

"She's got both," Grace grumbled. "Big boobs and a nice curvy ass."

Avery giggled. "Chelsey."

Their approaching critique set a flutter of nerves loose in my stomach. "She hardly compares to your curves."

"I know I got it in the trunk," Grace replied, her hips swinging wider, "but her perky double-D's are a visual stimuli even I can't compete with."

Avery and I did a simultaneous eye roll as I moved to the sink, distancing myself from the canvas and their reactions.

They both took it in at the same time and went silent, the ticking wall clock suddenly the loudest mechanism in the room. My palms turned damp. I plunged them under the spray of cold water, along with the brushes. Of all the art lessons I took in San Francisco, the one I never mastered was putting my art on display for public opinion.

It was Grace who finally broke the silence. "Couldn't you have at least distorted my boobs bigger?" she said of my version of Picasso's cubism using the two of them as models.

"I could have." The cold water bit at my hands as I cleaned the brushes. "But you both knew portraits weren't

my thing before I asked you to model."

"It was a stupid class assignment," Grace spit out.

Done with her 30-second scrutiny, she snagged a magazine off the art table and flopped herself down on the old couch along the wall. "But, as usual, yours turned out much better then my interpretation of the Seattle skyline."

Avery continued her thoughtful study of the canvas. "I don't get it."

"That's because it doesn't involve numbers or symbols," Grace quipped back to our math genius, whose interest in art ran just deep enough to put up with Grace and me.

My cell phone beeped as I dropped my brushes on the drying rack. I dried my hands and walked back to the art table, pushing around the clutter to find it. "So who's your source about Chelsey?"

"Jenni," Grace pouted.

"Unreliable," I said and moved up behind Avery who was still studying the canvas. "You don't have to look at it any longer," I whispered over her shoulder. "You've fulfilled your friendship viewing quotient."

"It's fascinating." She cocked her head left, than right. "I can see hints of me the longer I look at it, even though it looks nothing like me."

My phone beeped again.

"Girls. Focus. We're discussing me. What makes her unreliable?" Grace asked, stretching her legs out and flip-

ping through the magazine. I knew she was trying to act disinterested, but she wasn't fooling anyone.

"She's one of Chelsey's closest friends. She's just stirring the pot to see if anything floats to the top." I grabbed my phone and looked down at the screen. A text. From a number I didn't recognize.

"I agree," I heard Avery say as I stared at the number.

Finished with her analytical scrutiny, she moved over to the arm of the couch and added, "If you want an answer, you need to flush out a direct contender. Ask Chelsey."

"Or better yet," I said pulling up the text message, "you could ask . . ."

R U free Thursday night?
-Quentin

"I could ask who?" Grace's voice drifted into my scrambled confusion.

I reread the text, my heart hammering double-time in my chest. "You, um . . . could . . ." How did he get my cell phone number? I looked up at Grace, the only other person who knew Quentin existed. I wouldn't put it past her to prank me.

"What?" she asked.

"Where's your cell phone?"

She did a half roll and pulled it out of her back jean pocket. "Here. Why?"

"Never mind."

"Girl, you are losing it." She shoved her phone back in her pocket. "Are you going to answer my question?"

Staring at the text, I asked, "What question?"

"Focus, Cee. Focus. Who should I ask about Chelsey?"

"What? Oh, Sean." Distracted, I moved to the little bench seat in the window and hit the reply button, the dampness in my palms back. "You could ask Sean directly."

How did you get
this #?

"What do I care? Sean can date whomever he wants."

I shook my head, because I knew she did care. My phone beeped again, startling me.

If you're free on Thurs,
I'll tell you.

"CeeCee? Hello?" Grace's exaggerated voice catching my attention.

"What?" Annoyance seeped into my tone. I could easily sneak out, but to meet him? I looked out the window, picturing the car I saw drive-by earlier. I knew I needed to say no. I should say no. Every logical thought screamed no.

Grace lowered the magazine and shot me her best of-fended look. "Don't get uppity with me for asking you a friggin' question. Who's texting you, anyway?"

"Oh, um. Foster," I lied. "Complaining about his school work and lack of social life."

"It's his own fault," she shot back with her typical an-swer for everything. "Did your brother think he would be able to skate through an engineering degree?"

"Engineering's a great field," Avery added in.

"Whatever," Grace said, going back to her magazine. "But in my book, it's just another form of island isolation."

Island isolation. I was tired of isolation. Tired of this room. Tired of my own mind. Tired of gray. In a moment of irrational thought, I typed one word and hit send.

OK

"Not everything has to be about isolation," Avery add-ed. "It could just mean . . ."

The next beep seemed to have doubled in volume.

"CeeCee, I know you two are close and all, but you've got to cut him off."

I tuned her out to read the text.

Catch the 6:40 ferry.
I'll meet you on the other side.

I didn't reply. Unsure of what I'd just agreed to.

CHAPTER
7

"Can you believe that?" Dylan leaned over and asked after the last bell of the day released us from the apprehension I'd been locked in all week. "An essay? In French? By
next week? This class is going to kill me."

"Um, yeah." A French essay was the least of my worries. I was distracted by the fact that it was now Thursday
and I'd agreed to meet a total stranger in the city, who
may or may not be stalking me. Who may or may not be
a nice guy. Who may or may not . . .

Stop.

I had to stop with the what-ifs. I shoved my books
into my messenger bag and bee-lined for the door.

Dylan's lanky lope easily kept pace with my jumpy
gait. "Where are you off to? I told Grace and Avery I'd

meet them at the coffee shop after school. Do you want to come?"

I ignored the hope in his voice. "I can't."

We stepped into the mass of humanity that had flooded the halls. "I've got to, um . . . I've got some things I need to do." Like, go home and search for my sanity, which seemed to have vanished the moment I agreed to meet Quentin. Well, actually, before that, but I was now pushing the blame in his direction.

A body jarred my shoulder from behind and sent me tripping into Dylan. His French book fluttered to the ground as he awkwardly reached out to catch me and missed, leaving me to land with a "whoosh" on top of three hundred pages of *Français*.

"You okay?" He jammed the flow of bodies with his towering frame and reached down, clamping his clammy hands around my forearms, nearly yanking my arms from their sockets as he lifted me up against him.

"Yeah, fine." I quickly stepped back and shook my arms to be certain they were still attached and slung my bag back over my shoulder. "I've got to go."

He looked down at me hesitantly. I quickly looked away. "Um, okay, I guess I'll catch you later," he mumbled as his frame receded in the crowd.

I was too distracted to react to his tone and hesitation. I pushed my way against the flow, the jostling of bodies inflaming my anxiousness. Ignorance was my choice of

weapon against his unasked questions of interest. I didn't ask for it, and I sure didn't encourage it. I wanted nothing that would tie me to this island come the end of the school year.

The doors to the north parking lot were in sight. I could almost taste the fresh air on the other side. My body slugged through the last ten feet.

"CeeCee!"

Cut short of opening the door, I turned to see Grace running to catch up with me.

Winded, she asked, "Can I get a ride to the coffee shop?"

"Where's your car?" An endless afternoon of Grace chit-chat was not what I needed. Inevitably, my focus, or lack of, would be called into question, leading to a relentless inquiry as to why.

She followed on my tail out the door. "In the repair shop again. I should have opted for an oldie like yours."

I sucked in a deep breath. With every step, the cool air sliced through my lungs, expelling bits of pent-up anxiety.

"Besides," she continued, "you could stand a few moments out of that fume filled room of yours," she added.

"I've just got some stuff to do." I set my messenger bag on the hood of my car and began the endless search for car keys.

Undeterred by my "no," she walked around to the passenger door and waited. "What stuff?"

"Is this an interrogation?" I glanced irritably over the top of my car. "If you must know, I have a hot date in the city I have to get ready for."

She held her laughter back for all of two seconds before letting it rip. "Girlfriend, you are funny." She was actually snorting. "You've given no island misfit the time of day, and now, one in the city? I don't think so. You're not that good at keeping secrets from me."

That's what she thought. We both slid into my car at the same time. "I said I wasn't going to the coffee shop."

"I know, but you can still roll your little ride by and drop me off." She wasn't getting out. I relented and backed out of my parking spot. "So, speaking of dates, Avery and I decided we should all go to Homecoming together as a group."

I glanced at her, trying to assess where this was leading. "Have fun."

"You'll come." She flipped down the visor and began a lip-gloss and primp routine. "It's totally casual. We figure we can all watch the game together and then head to the dance. Dylan's coming too."

"Is Sean coming?"

"The last time I checked, we lived in a free country. No one's stopping him." I could have puckered from her tartness. She tossed her gloss back in her bag, asking, "So, you'll come?"

I pulled into the coffee shop parking lot and left my car idling, "Don't know."

"I'm not getting out of the car until you agree to go."

"Get out. I'll come." I caved easily, figuring I'd work on an excuse when my brain was less occupied by near future events.

"Goodbye to you, too." She slammed the door closed and sashayed up the stairs to the coffee shop.

CHAPTER
8

Locked in the safety of my bedroom, I pulled open my closet and stared, daunted by the clothes hanging in the tight space. I didn't want to care. I reached for a clean shirt to replace the one I was wearing, but instead, my hand landed on a hanger holding a black flippy skirt. I pulled it out, but quickly shoved it back in. Too much.

An instant later, I pulled it out again and threw it on. Along with an emerald green cardigan and boots.

I stepped in front of the mirror, a long sigh escaped up my throat. Who was I kidding?

I grabbed a rubber band and pulled my hair partly up in the back, trying to hide the out of control natural of the kinks. My hands dropped to my side and I stared. I didn't have to go. No one was holding a gun to my head.

I could just stay home, not get on the ferry, never see him again.

Distraction. I needed a distraction. And to stop looking in the mirror. Grace would have been the perfect distraction. Her voice would fill every crevice in my head. But even she would eventually circle back around, inflaming my already fire of nerves with questions.

My eyes landed on my French book. The essay. Perfect. Foreign words to run interference with spools of crazy English thoughts. I didn't get far when there was a light knock on the door.

"Come in," I said not looking up, assuming it was Dad.

"Hello, Miss CeeCee."

The chimes of Aunt Lucy's voice tingled the air as she breezed through the door, her peasant skirt swishing gently around her long, slender legs. "I was in the neighborhood and thought I would stop by to see how you all were getting along."

I spun my desk chair around, grateful for the unplanned distraction. "Same as always. And you?"

"Oh, fine." Her eyes wandered up and down me, the waves of her long, dusty brown hair brushing the top of her tailbone. "Don't you look nice? Is dressing up a requirement for doing homework?"

Consciously, my hands brushed down my skirt, tucking the ends tight around my legs. "Um, well, yes, as a matter of fact, it is."

"Mmm." A single eyebrow lifted slightly as she moved further into my room. "Any other reason for dressing up?"

"Nope, not that I know of." The guilt of the lie landed like a rock in the pit of my stomach. I could tell her. Of all people, I could tell her. My hesitation hung briefly before I knew I wouldn't. "Unless you wanted to take me out on the town."

"Probably not tonight, but I'd be happy to another time." She stood in front of my dresser, her fingers danced lightly over the items cluttered on top. "The girls mentioned they hadn't seen you around school recently."

"I've been around. I just don't have hair that makes me easily noticeable."

Aunt Lucy's fourteen year old twin daughters, Autumn and Summer, were both topped with the brightest red hair imaginable, although their sameness in looks were punctuated by opposite dispositions.

"Did you enjoy your night at the Picasso show?" she asked.

Did she know? Did she talk to Evelyn? "It was, um, fun," I stuttered and tried to change the subject. "Ms. Harris had us do a Picasso-esque assignment for class."

She looked at me, and I was certain my truth withholding slid across her eyes knowingly. She reached out and lifted a framed picture of my mom off the top of the dresser. My favorite. The camera shutter had stolen a moment and perfectly captured her essence. Her bare

feet were tucked deep in the sand, and a beautiful floral sundress hung stylishly over her lithe frame. Her mouth was curved wide, her head tossed back, and you could almost hear her laughter swirling in the salt air.

"Gretta was a beautiful woman, Cee." She gently set the frame down and turned back to me. "I see much of her in you."

The compliment stung the back of my eyes. I swallowed down the loss, bit my tongue, and muttered, "Thanks."

CHAPTER
9

Aunt Lucy's presence proved damaging to my psyche, leaving me befuddled and late as I slipped down the stairs and muttered a "studying at Grace's house" excuse to Dad.

"Not a late night!" was all I heard as the door clicked closed behind me.

My Ghia whirled like a bee as I raced to the ferry, certain I would miss it. At the moment, I didn't care. The evening had turned into a mental game of damage control, reining Mom's memory in tight enough for me to deal with the uncertainty of what waited on the other side of the water.

I pulled into the commuter lot and ran down to the idling ferry, thankful I only had to pay for the crossing when boarding on the Seattle side.

"Good timing," the ferry worker said as I stepped aboard. "You're the last." He pulled a rope across the back of the boat, ending all other racers from boarding.

The engines roared to life and boiled the water into a frothy foam of mint green. The same green that washed ashore behind my mom in the picture on my dresser. For a split-second, the two scenes merged and the spirit of my mother circled the air around me. I stood, not wanting the trance to end as my hair whipped around in a childish game of peek-a-boo with the receding dock. But with every breath I sucked down, the boat floated further and further from the dock, vibrating the foam into soft rings of murky green. My isolation solidified.

Not a soul knew where I was, save one.

Chilled, I staggered up the stairs into the protection of the cabin and dropped down into a booth near the front. The city was a blaze of golden brilliance. The autumn sunset shimmered back like fire against the towering skyline. It was stunning, blinding — thawing my chills of uncertainty until the ferry horn blew and jolted my body to attention, the Seattle terminal within striking distance.

Trepidation kept my pace slow as I crossed the upper deck, my heart pounding in my ears. I merged into the folds of the other people congregated on the small outer deck as we waited for the foot passenger bridge to be lowered into place, the warmth of bodies a false solidarity.

What was I doing?

I jostled forward with the group and walked the plank before we stepped through the first set of doors. My breath caught as I spied him leaning casually against a post in the back of the room. I watched him look for me, only the subtle movement of his dark hair giving away his search. Dark, inky waves that perfectly framed the lines of his face.

Our eyes connected instantly as I stepped through the second set of doors. Everything came to a silent standstill. Vanishing. Only the sound of my blood pulsing behind my ears interrupted the frozen scene.

Quentin pushed off the post, his steps deliberate, closing the gap between us.

"CeeCee . . ." he hesitated inches from me, as if not knowing what to say.

My mind stumbled in a panic and blurted out the first nervous thought it latched on to. "How did you get my number?"

His mouth pulled into a tight line. He put his hand behind my elbow and moved us out of the flow of passengers coming off the ferry. A patch of heat blossomed from his touch sending zings of electricity up my arm as he guided us out of the terminal. We followed the crowd to an outside breezeway and continued across a footbridge that led to First Avenue.

His silence was deafening in the loud city. "You said if I was free tonight, you would tell me how you got my number."

Leading us south on First Avenue through a small triangle shaped park, he finally broke his silence. "Yes, but the night is not over."

"It's about to be." I quit walking, breaking his grip from my elbow as I stopped on a corner under a large L-shaped scrolling iron bus stop. A glass canopy bubbled through the hard lines of metal, reminiscent of another time.

He turned and stared down at me, his sharp green eyes prickling a layer of unease across my skin. "How do you know Eveyln?"

The question caught me off guard. My defenses soared. Unable to hold his cold gaze, I turned my head and said, "I don't."

"That's odd," his voice filled with sarcasm, "according to the SAM guest list, there were two Vanderbie's in attendance the night of the Picasso show."

My head started to spin. Is this why he invited me? So he could call me a liar to my face? "Is that part of your job description? Guest list screening?"

He didn't answer.

My eyes traced the scrolls of the iron structure, following it to the canopy, the last of the golden sunset rippling across the glass. "What is this thing? Is this a bus stop?"

My eyes were back to him.

The question threw him off, uncorking whatever steam he'd built up. "It's not a bus stop. It's a pergola, built in the late 1800's." His own eyes softened as he took

in the structure.

"And you know this because . . ."

"Because I went on the Underground tour." Finished with the distraction, he asked again, "How do you know Eveyln?"

"So, what's underground and why would one go down there?"

The light changed and he guided us across the street. "What's left of Pioneer Square after a fire in the late 1800s." I was about to make a sarcastic crack, but he circled us back one more time. "Why did Evelyn ask me to introduce you to her?"

"Because I'd never met her before," I said in hopes of ending his questioning. "You still haven't told me how you got my number."

"Are you telling me that it's a coincidence that you have the same last name?"

Deflated, my shoulders dropped and I softly replied, "No, it's not a coincidence. She's my grandmother."

"Did you not know you had a grandmother?" I could hear the skepticism in his voice.

"I knew, but we'd never met before that night." I couldn't look at him, embarrassed to be talking about my family garbage, which, even I didn't understand. I looked around and noticed more people walking up and down the streets. "Are we done? Because the rest of this story would take more minutes then are left in the night."

The pause was long, but he finally answered, "For now."

"Where are we going anyway?"

"It's First Thursday art walk," he said as we walked deeper into the Pioneer Gallery District. "I thought you might like to see some art."

Dubious, I looked up and asked, "Was this before or after you found out my last name was Vanderbie?"

"Before." I wasn't so sure, but he didn't ask any more questions.

CHAPTER
10

We spent the next few hours walking in and out of galleries. Our debates lingered safely on the context of art. Around the truths and lies, the real and the make believe, the good and the evil.

One artist in particular, an oil painter, held us both captive. His small canvases forced us to step close while the minute details grabbed hold, daring us to look harder, to follow the lines off the canvas and search for what treasures lay hidden underneath.

I was completely consumed. So much so, I didn't notice when Quentin had stepped outside, his dark silhouette reflecting through the front window, his hand holding a cell phone to his ear. I weaved through the other art viewers, unintentionally shivering as I crossed into the chilly evening air. Quentin's eyes followed my every

movement. He ended his call as I neared, and pulled his coat off, draping it around my shoulders. He was everywhere. The musky scent of him rising all around me. Every sense in my body heightened.

"There are two more galleries on the next street over," his voice soft in the night air. "Do you have time?"

"Sure." I had no idea what time it was, but I knew I wasn't ready to go home. I looked up to his face and quietly asked, "Are you going to tell me how you got my phone number?"

"Does it matter?"

"No, not really."

We started to walk down the street, when his low voice murmured, "Evelyn."

Of course, Evelyn. How she had my number, I have no idea.

Washed in a scent of contentment, we rounded the corner and crossed a street cutting a diagonal path across the otherwise traditional city grid. It was a short, odd street, which abruptly came to an end at the mouth of an alleyway. The dark opening pulled me like a magnet and I was unable to stop my feet from moving toward their new trajectory.

"CeeCee, the galleries are this way."

It began, like it always began, at the base of my neck.

Please, not tonight, I thought.

For weeks I'd waited, prepared myself for the onslaught, almost convinced myself I'd imagined the entire

thing. But tonight, I let down my guard and now my mind would pay the consequence.

I heard Quentin's voice somewhere behind me, but with every step, the penetrating needles grew stronger. Forcing me to focus. Preparing me for what was about to unleash. And unleash it did. Slow at first, like a freight train picking up speed, until my entire mind was coated in color. Blues of every shade, bending into red.

I knew enough not to be fooled by the beauty, because it was always followed by horror.

"CeeCee, where are you going?"

I wanted to turn to him, but the colors blew out like a candle, and my mind was ravished by exploding images.

The outline of a man.

The silhouette of a couple.

The flash of a gun.

Faster and faster they shuffled, casting me into depths of darkness as the silent movie came to life. A shadowy man next to a dumpster. A couple. The flash of a gun. Spinning blue lights throbbing hues of gray over the entire scene.

On they went. Fear booming inside of me, adding the only soundtrack to the scene.

The shadowy man by the dumpster.

The backs of the couple.

The gun.

The blue lights.

I stood at the mouth of the alley. My eyes open, unseeing, my body shaking uncontrollably. I felt Quentin's arm wrap firmly around my back. I wanted to spin into him, to force my eyes from the unfolding scene.

"CeeCee?" A whisper, a lifeline, in the storm of silence, in the nightmare playing out in front of me. The images continued to march forward. One after the other.

The man.

The couple.

The flash of a gun muzzle.

Until one image burst forward and hovered. It dangled over me, crushing me under its weight. A single silhouette, crumpled on the ground, bathed in blue light, begging me to understand.

"Stop!" I screamed. I grabbed the sides of my head, tears streaming down my cheeks. "No more! Please, no more!"

And like a T.V. unplugged from the wall, they immediately vanished, leaving only a heavy gray fog over my mind.

My body fell under the pressure of their hasty retreat, but not before Quentin's arms wrapped protectively around my waist, safely holding my feet to solid ground. My eyes darted in panic, looking for the couple. For the man. But all that remained was a cold, dark alley, just as it was when I first noticed it, trails of dumpsters as far as the eye could see.

"CeeCee?" Quentin probed again. He grabbed my shoulders and spun me to him, away from the trail of darkness. His hands clasped over my cheeks, rubbing life back into them with his fingers, forcing me to look in his eyes, which I feared could see clearly into my slipping mind. "You have to tell me what's going on."

"I don't know." My skin prickled in a sweaty chill. "My mind . . .um . . . I saw . . ."

I looked back over my shoulder at the alley, but nothing was amiss. There was no one but us. I felt the dam behind my eyes threatening to break as I turned back to Quentin. To his eyes. The concern floating in them was my undoing, unleashing a torrent of tears. My chin dropped as my shoulders burst up and down with every jagged breath I sucked in. Quentin pulled me to him.

This can't be happening, this can't be happening, spun over and over in my mind like a broken record, holding back all irrational explanations. I sunk deeper into the warmth of his arms, which kept me from splitting in two.

Time marched forward and slowed my breath into small hiccups.

"Did you see something? Like at the dock?"

I nodded into his chest, unable to trust my voice. Unable to trust that the lingering tingles wouldn't return with a vengeance.

"Let's get out of here," he whispered calmly, as if what was happening to me was an every day occurrence.

I pushed him away, fear roaring in me like a bear. "Why are you so calm? Why aren't you freaking out? I'm seriously losing it. Sliding off the mental deep-end."

I watched the shutters come down over the concern in his eyes, making me wonder if I'd imagined that too. "Trust me, this is nowhere near the deep-end."

"What?" I howled. "What does that mean?"

He reached for my elbow and walked us away from the alley. "Nothing."

"Nothing?" I stepped out of his touch and tried to calm the frenzy building inside me, the fear that my mind was slipping in front of him. Always in front of him. The new thought spewed out an irrational accusation. "You're the reason this is happening."

Affronted, he threw up his hands and said, "I have no idea what you are talking about."

"I have no idea either. All I know is, every time you're around, I start seeing things." I turned and stumbled in the direction I thought the ferry would be. I had to get out of here. Away from him.

"CeeCee. Where are you going?"

"Home!" I snapped, my feet tripping a jagged line down the sidewalk.

Quentin ran up behind me and grabbed my arm. "Stop, CeeCee. Talk to me."

I threw my finger in his face. "Were you on the island Monday? Did you drive by my house?"

"CeeCee, I think you need to calm down."

"Were you there?" I asked in near hysterics. "Are you stalking me?"

Quentin grabbed for my hand. "CeeCee, what happened? What did you see?"

"Someone was shot," I yelled. My body shook uncontrollably with the revelation.

His recoiled and dropped my hand. "What do you mean 'someone was shot'?"

I couldn't stop the tremors inside me, forcing me to gulp for air as I tried to explain. "I saw the outline of a man and a couple. A gun went off. I saw the flash of a gun."

Quentin didn't reply. One minute turned into another and I started to panic. I didn't want him to think I was crazy. I wasn't crazy! I lifted my head to see if I could read his face, but the darkness covered his features in shadows, leaving them unattainable.

I couldn't stand his silent scrutiny any longer. "I'm losing it, aren't I? I'm fucking losing my mind."

He looked at me, his eyes murky pools on a mask I couldn't read. The ferry horn filled the air and he jerked his head in the direction of the boat and pushed us forward. "We should get you on that boat."

That's right. Send the crazy girl back into isolation.

The ferry terminal was nearly vacant. Quentin stepped up to the ticket window and said, "Two foot passengers."

"You don't have to cross over," I protested as he finished the transaction.

He grabbed the tickets from the window agent and marched us into the holding area.

Hating his silence more than his patronizing actions, I snapped, "I can take care of myself. I don't need to be handled like a child."

"I don't doubt it," he fumed, the hard lines of his face sinking a little deeper. "But since you have no idea what just happened and you really don't know how deep the deep-end really is, a little forbearance would be acceptable while I make sure you get to your car safely."

What was that supposed to mean? A little forbearance? I wanted to ask, but I was exhausted, unable to endure any more question and answer sessions.

We boarded and I walked straight to the booth I'd ridden over in a lifetime ago. Quentin sat next to me, releasing a current of electricity down my left side. It washed over me, soothing, melting down my hardening stance. Together, we sat quietly, side by side, until the ferry reached Vashon. He followed behind me to the commuter parking lot.

"Is this your car?" Quentin asked as I stepped up to the red Ghia, it's white convertible top glowing in the dim light.

"Yes," my defensive posture back. "Is there a problem with it?"

"No, no." He held his hands up. "Just a surprising choice."

"Well, I didn't choose it. I inherited it from my dead mom," I unfairly spit out to rattle him.

"I'm sorry." His voice dropped low and velvety, slipping in and around the pain. "You'd better go before your dad worries."

I handed him his coat, a chill shuddering through me as I got in my car. "Not something I have to worry about."

I reached out to pull the door closed, but Quentin stepped in its closing path and pushed it wider, leaning in. The air was suddenly sucked gone. I held my breath.

Breathe. Breathe.

Hesitation lingered, his eyes locked on mine, before he said, "Goodnight," and slammed the door closed, vanishing into the dark.

CHAPTER
11

I snatched my bag from my locker, thankful it was Friday. Thankful to escape the torturous day I'd forced myself to move through. But no amount of school distraction was able to shake the cold feeling left in the wake of last night's images. It was a war of shadows dueling in my mind, tormenting me to understand their vagueness before they'd made a hasty retreat into nothingness. I had no idea why my mind conjured up the people, but was fairly certain their fate did not end well.

I cut through the back doors of the school, instantly wrapped in a veil of mist. My mind felt like a scarlet "A" that throbbed for all to see the craziness lurking behind my eyes. I picked up my pace as I wove in and out of the parked cars, my cell phone beeping somewhere in the depths of my messenger bag. I dug for my keys and came

up with my phone. I ducked into the car, wiped the mist from my eyes, and glanced at the screen. My stomach clenched as the letters of Quentin's name sprung from the screen, along with three words:

Where R U?

The brusqueness of his message sent annoyance down my spine. What does he mean, where am I? What business is it of his?

Why? Where R U?

I tossed the phone on the seat and pulled out of the parking spot. The beep was instantaneous. I stopped and picked it up.

In UR house

My heart hiccupped in disbelief as I re-read the text. This had to be a joke. A very bad joke.

A horn blared behind me, causing me to jump. I looked in the rearview mirror and saw a line of cars stacking up behind me. I tossed the phone back to the passenger seat and slammed on the gas, racing away from the school at record speed.

My grip on the steering wheel tightened in anger. The nerve, showing up uninvited. He had no right to be

there, to be sharing anything with my dad. I wrenched the steering wheel hard into my driveway and skidded to a stop in front of Quentin's parked car. My shoulders slumped. It wasn't a joke. He was inside my house, telling Dad who knows what.

This day was not going to end well.

The mist had upgraded to a full rain shower by the time I ran up the front steps and burst through the door, my eyes adjusting to the unreal scene before me: Quentin and Dad were sitting quietly across from one another in the living room.

"Cee? Is that you?" Dad asked, standing up from his spot on the couch.

"Yes." I skirted cautiously around the backside of the furniture like a trapped prey, not taking my eyes off of Quentin.

His eyes held mine in a contest that was becoming all too familiar. I braced myself, waiting for the questions, the accusations.

Instead, Dad said, "Quentin Stone is here from the University as part of the art partnering program you forgot to mention to me." His disapproval rang loud. Picking up his cane, he moved to a familiar spot at the end of the couch where he could be sure of where he was looking.

Partnering program? What the . . .?

Quentin stood, a newspaper tucked under his arm. "Your art teacher, Ms. Harris, passed along your contact

information to me so we could meet," Quentin lied with ease as he walked toward me. He stretched out his hand in a friendly gesture, but the gesture didn't touch his frosty emeralds. "It's nice to finally meet you, CeeCee. My name is Quentin Stone."

I had no idea what was going on.

I hesitated before shaking his hand and prayed it would not end with me on the floor. "Um, nice to meet you Quentin." My feet remained firmly on the ground. The warmth of his grip crawled up my arm, skewing the moment and tipping it sideways. Sarcasm drifted into my tone as I added, "It was lucky for you that you knew Ms. Harris, and she could connect us."

"Yes, it was convenient, wasn't it? Would you like to show me any of the current art pieces you're working on?" He didn't relinquish my hand, but continued to hold it firm in his grip.

I looked over at Dad anxiously, waiting for him to react. Waiting for him to toss Quentin out. Waiting for him to say something. Anything. "Um, sure. I have some in the room above the garage."

I yanked my hand from his and turned to walk out of the room. Dad finally broke his silence — two minutes too late. "Cee, when you're done, will you please come back in and find me?"

"Okay." I didn't bother to look at him, or wait to see if Quentin would follow. Instead, I stalked out the front door into the rain, my words locked in my throat where

anger bubbled close to the surface. I tucked my head down and picked up my pace as I crossed over the wet gravel, Quentin's feet falling somewhere close behind me.

"Is your dad the deranged person wandering around your house?" His voice traveled over my shoulder and ran into my wall of irritation.

"Amongst other things," I said, simmering as I climbed the stairs to the art room two at a time.

"He appeared lucid to me."

"Appearances can be deceiving," I snapped and wiped the rain off my face. The sharp scent of acrylic paint greeted me as I stepped into my sanctuary and moved to the far side of the art table, happy for the barrier between us.

His voice turned serious. "Has he always been blind?"

The tragic story of my family was not a journey I had the energy to take today. "Why are you here Quentin, and what the hell is the 'partnering program'?"

He closed the door and spun the newspaper he'd had lodged under his arm across the art table. The damp pages came to a stop in front of me, an article circled in red facing up.

"What's this?"

"Read it," his hard voice urged, leaving no room for argument.

Mugging in Pioneer Square Leaves One Dead
Seattle, WA: Karen and Leland Tate were held at gunpoint around 1:00am Friday morning,

while crossing through an alley in the Pioneer Square area of Seattle. An unknown assailant came out from the alley, demanding the Tates' purse and wallet. When they didn't immediately surrender their money, the husband was shot twice in the chest. The police are asking for any information in regards to the shooting. The assailant is still at large.

I was stunned. I read the story three times, the shadows in my mind aligning to the words on the page. My breathing turned into huge heaves. I couldn't look at him. "This could be anybody," I choked out, the walls of my sanctuary pressing in around me.

"It could be." He crept gradually around the table, rendering the barrier useless.

"It's not what you think." Panic sprung loose. I grabbed the edge of the art table and tried to suck in the non-existent air in the room. "It can't be."

"How could you possibly know what I'm thinking?" His voice was eerily calm, causing my loose panic to strangle my rational thought.

"IT'S NOT!" I trembled from head to toe. This couldn't be happening. My eyes darted around, looking for anything that felt normal. Anything that resembled my life before my mom died. Before we moved. Before Quentin.

Unable to control my breathing, I bent over and put my hands on my knees. I was determined not to pass out.

Again.

Quentin moved up next to me, demanding answers. "Do you know what I'm thinking? Or can you only see . . ."

"Don't say it," I interrupted so he couldn't finish his sentence. I lifted myself upright too quickly, causing the massive amount of blood in my head to trip up my balance. Quentin reached out to steady me, but I pulled away, working to control the wave of tears threatening to escape. "You can't say it."

"I need an explanation." His tone was chilling, his face a mask of intimidation. "Now!"

"I don't know what you're talking about."

"The lost girl in the dark routine is getting old, CeeCee," he hissed, taking a step closer. "What kind of game are you playing at? People are dead."

He was searching my face for an answer, but I had none. No answer racing through my mind seemed remotely plausible.

The rain continued its assault on the roof and filled the painful quiet.

Moments.

Ticking.

He pointed to the newspaper lying accusingly on the art table. "How were you able to see that shooting before it happened?"

"I already told you, what I saw was too fuzzy," I sputtered. "They were shadows acting out a play with no

lights or sounds. It could have been anyone."

"Which means, it could have been the Tates."

"Oh, no." I recoiled from his words. "THAT is not even remotely possible. That is something that only happens in teen vampire novels."

"I've known you for what, a month? And it has already happen three times. Three times you've nearly passed out from seeing random visions."

"They. Are. NOT. VISIONS." I was unwilling to venture down this slippery slope of possibility.

"How do you know?"

"Because nothing like this ever happened before I met you," I said as I grasped onto my thin accusations of last night. "It's you. Maybe you're the one causing this to happen to me."

"You do not want to mess with me." His tone turned deadly. My heart threatened to thump out of my chest. "I moved to Seattle to get away from idiots and lies, and crap like this. The last thing I need is your fucking mind trip."

"Me? Mess with YOU? No one asked you to come here today," I spit out defensively, backing toward the window. "No one asked you to lie to my dad. Or, invite me on the art walk. Or heap your stupid opinions on me at the SAM. That. Was. All. YOU!"

"What the hell are you doing to me?" The words were barely audible as he pushed both his hands through the dark waves of his hair. I wasn't even certain they were meant for me. With renewed vigor, his eyes darkened

and pierced through me. "From the moment I saw you staring all teary eyed at those Picasso women, I knew something was off. Every instinct told me to ignore you and your strange, not normal . . .I don't know what." His hands flailed the air in front of him. "But every time I did, a hard, nagging feeling of dread took over, leaving me overwhelmed with the need to check on you."

Hurt by his words I knew as truth, *"strange, not normal,"* my throat strangled my voice silent. There was no way to recap this spinning bottle of truth.

I dropped down on the bench seat in the window and pulled my legs up tight against my chest. I leaned my head against the glass, streaks of rain sliding past my eyes, rolling time forward. I wanted it to stop. To run backward. To erase the art walk, the alley, the images from my mind. To erase the warmth I felt sitting next to Quentin on the ferry.

"Are you psychic?" he asked, interrupting my thoughts. "Can you read minds?"

"No." I wanted to laugh at the absurdity of the question.

"Can you see into the past?" There was an edge to the question.

"No," I whispered under my breath. I rested my chin on my knees, my arms wrapped tight around my legs in an attempt to keep them from extending and running out the door.

"Are you sure this has never happened before the night at the SAM?"

I nodded my head yes, too drained to say anything more. Too scared I might break down. I would not cry. I would not give him the satisfaction of knowing he got to me.

"Does anyone else know about this?"

Something inside me snapped. "No. No. And no. I can't read minds. I can't see the past or the future. I can't cast spells over people and make them seek me out against their will. And yes, you are the only privileged soul to know I'm slowly sliding myself into a straight jacket. Any other questions?"

He was momentarily stunned by my outburst before he closed the distance between us with five purposeful strides. My back went rigid, bracing for another round of accusations. Before I could react to his movement, he was in front of me, his hand stretched out, softly caressing my cheekbone with his thumb.

The gesture was so unexpected, my head automatically leaned into his palm. Into the caress. Into his touch. The intimacy washed over my uncertainty. Ever so smoothly, he pulled me up to my feet and into his arms, my senses overwhelmed by his musky scent and the warmth shooting up and down my spine.

Softly, over my racing heart, I heard him say, "Cee, I don't know what to think. I don't know what's happen-

ing." There was frustration in his voice. My arms dangled, unsure of how to react. "Every instinct inside of me says I should leave and walk out that door."

And yet, here he was.

I didn't answer. I stood perfectly still. I knew we were teetering on a precarious edge that could give way at any moment.

And give way it did. With the single ring of Quentin's cell phone. He released me, swearing under his breath, and had his cell phone to his ear before a second ring sounded off.

"Yes?" he barked, turning his back to me as he walked to the other side of the room.

I dropped down on the bench, trying to decide if what just happened really happened.

"No, not yet," he said to whomever he was talking to. He glanced over at me and I quickly diverted my eyes.

"I said I would take care of it, " he hissed irritable, abruptly ending the conversation. He ran his hand through his hair again and turned to look at me. "I have to go."

"Someone else needing to be checked on?" I didn't move from my place by the window.

His hand hesitated on the doorknob. "Um, I'll call you."

But I didn't believe it any more than he did.

CHAPTER

12

I walked back to the house in a dreary stupor.

"CeeCee?"

Dad. I'd forgotten about Dad. I trudged into the living room and found him sitting ramrod straight on the couch, his cane hovering vertically between his legs.

"Yeah?" I moved behind the chair next to the couch, exhaustion and water dripping from every limb of my body.

His eyes found my voice, eerily looking but not seeing me. "CeeCee, I do not think it is appropriate for Ms. Harris to be passing out our personal information to a complete stranger."

"She didn't." I scrambled to come up with a logical explanation so he wouldn't try to contact her. "When I signed up for the, um, partnering program, I said she

could give my information to whomever she thought I would partner best with."

"You should have told me about the program. Your school should have sent information home about the program and what was to be expected."

If they did, I doubt he would have read it. "It's no big deal. They were just trying to connect artists up."

He stood, agitated. "It is still inappropriate to have an unknown male show up at our house and you spend time alone with him in that room of yours above the garage."

"Dad, seriously," embarrassed by his train of thought. "He's just a photography student at the U."

"He told me that much. But he was too quiet. Nobody is that quiet. You know nothing about him . . ."

Irritation flared up at his sudden need to be a parent. "Dad," I gritted out, "it's no big deal."

"It is a big deal. I may not be able to see, but I can hear. And there were times I couldn't even hear him breathe."

"Well, that's something," I added hotly and turned to leave the room. "Because at times I've wondered if you were still breathing."

"CeeCee, you are seventeen and still living under my roof and my rules," his raised voice countered, but he didn't bother to try and follow me out of the room. "I am still your father and you will speak to me with respect."

"Hmph," I grunted.

Father. He hadn't been a father since the day Mom died. Since the day he couldn't gain control of the car,

spinning everything about our lives into this mess. He was the reason we were here.

I headed up the stairs, and stormed down the upstairs hallway that overlooked the living room.

"And don't forget we have dinner at Lucy's in thirty minutes," he added distastefully.

Ugh. My head had no space for an evening with the cousins. Why he ever bothered to accept her invitations was beyond me. Everything about his sister rubbed him wrong. She was the only decent thing left in our lives and he managed to push her away every chance he got.

I glanced over the banister and caught sight of him standing directly in front of the only art piece of Mom's that he'd kept. She'd made a name for herself in San Francisco, but Dad had sold all her paintings, save one. His arm was stretched out, his fingers tracing the contours of the metal pieces folded gently into the waves of linen, the background flooded in an ocean of blue.

It was breathtaking. No. Heartbreaking.

I knew he was trying to touch Mom, to find her energy in the raging ocean background. I tore my intruding eyes away. The intimacy of the moment produced a wave of grief, of loss, of guilt for having lashed out at him.

CHAPTER
13

The drive to Aunt Lucy's was quiet.

No mention of Quentin, or the partnering program, or our fight. A stark contrast to the wall of sound we were greeted with as Summer opened the door and her mouth at the same time.

"CeeCee!" Summer threw her arms around me, my mouth catching a clump of her bright red hair. My body sagged, unsure if I could force myself through an evening with the twins after the emotional roller coaster of the past twenty-four hours.

"Hey, Summer," I said, spitting her hair out of my mouth. I pulled away and noticed Autumn standing quietly behind her. "Hi, Autumn."

"Girls," Dad added gruffly as he shuffled by us and into Aunt Lucy and Uncle Russell's ultimate "great

room" themed house. There were no doors, only partial walls that crisscrossed each other giving you the illusion of privacy.

"Well, he's in a fine mood," Summer whispered behind her hand, but I'm certain he had heard her.

"Summer, why don't you let CeeCee actually enter the house," Autumn stated matter-of-factly over her shoulder as she followed behind Dad. I liked Autumn and her brusque ways.

"I am. Sheez." She slapped the door closed and looped her arm through mine like we were the best of friends. "It's been forever. I can't remember the last time we saw you."

"Last week at school," I answered, which didn't seem all that long ago to me.

"Welcome, Peter," I heard Uncle Russell say to my dad. "Would you like to join me out on the back porch while I fire up the grill?"

"Russell, Peter does not want to sit out there in the cold and smoke," Aunt Lucy chastised before saying, "Hello, Peter."

I rounded the corner in time to see the half-hearted hug my dad reciprocated to his sister's embrace.

"Sure he does," Russell answered, his ill-matching outfit enhanced by the dark socks sticking out of his sandals. Dad remained quiet. "Otherwise he'll have to listen to all of you ladies prattle on about who knows what."

"I'll join you, Russell," Dad answered, putting his hand on Russell's shoulder, allowing him to lead him out to the deck.

My aunt walked over and gave me a hug. "How are you, my dear?"

"Fine." My tone was flat, but so was my mood.

"That's it? Just fine?" She held my shoulders and bent down to look directly in my eyes.

"It's been a long day. So yes, 'just fine' about sums it up."

She hesitated a moment longer, an uncertainty crossing over her eyes before she said, "I'm almost done in the kitchen and then I will come join you girls."

"Do you need any help?" I asked, hoping to avoid a painful dose of Summer's vomit of the mouth.

"No, no. I'm about done. You sit and enjoy yourself." She walked back to the kitchen, which was only separated from the room by a breakfast bar with four stools sitting in front of it.

I dropped down on the couch and Summer pounced down next to me. Autumn was already curled up in an oversized chair with her nose in a book.

"So," Summer hummed with a gleam in her eye. "Who is he?"

"Who's who?" I asked, having no idea what she was talking about.

"The guy? The dark haired guy?"

The tempo of my heart picked up. She couldn't know. There's no way she could know. "What dark haired guy are you talking about?" I asked again, trying to play it cool, praying none of this conversation was floating out of the room. "There are so many, after all."

"Summer, lay off," Autumn said from behind her book. "If she wants you to know, she'll tell you."

Ignoring her sister, Summer went on. "Natalie McDonald said she saw you hanging out with some dark haired guy she didn't recognize down at Point Robinson Lighthouse."

How did I not see Natalie? I don't remember seeing anyone. I hate small towns and small islands. My mind was spinning for a plausible answer to divert Summer from her current track of thinking. "Oh, him," I said as casually as I could make my voice sound. "He was some photography student asking about other parks on the island."

"Does he go to Vashon High?" she probed relentlessly, her eyes hoping for something juicy.

"No," I said, glancing up at Autumn, whose attention was caught by something behind me. "He's a student over in Seattle."

"Who's a student in Seattle?" Aunt Lucy's voice floated by. I turned my head, cringing inside.

"A photography student that CeeCee was hanging out with last weekend at Point Robinson Lighthouse," Summer graciously answered.

"I wasn't hanging out with him," trying to clarify over the heavy pounding in my chest. "He just came up to me and asked for directions."

"Mmm," Aunt Lucy breathed before saying, "Girls, could you please finish setting the table? Dinner is almost ready."

"I can help," I said, standing up.

"No, they can take care of it." She gestured for me to sit back down next to her on the couch.

"A Seattle student?" she asked, resting her arm on the back of the coach. "Anyone you might dress up for to do homework with?"

"I really don't know him." I stared off, unable to look her in the eyes. "Summer jumped to the wrong conclusion. I ran into him while I was down at the park and he asked about other places to shoot photos of long, dark shadows."

She placed her fingers under my chin and lifted until her intense gaze held mine. "If there was someone you were dressing up for, you could tell me," she said gently. "I know I'm not Gretta, but I'm pretty good at boy talk."

"There's no one." The first of my words that weren't a lie.

"Dinner is off the grill," Uncle Russell bellowed from the kitchen. I worked hard to contain my sigh of relief.

I was about to stand, when Aunt Lucy said, "The girls and I are planning a trip into the city on Sunday. Would you have any interest in joining us?"

My brain hurt. I couldn't come up with an excuse fast enough to get out of going. "Okay."

"Wonderful." She wrapped her arm around my shoulder and led me toward the kitchen. "We'll be glad to have your company."

CHAPTER
14

"Too much?" Grace asked turning back and forth in front of her mirror, admiring the fifth top she'd tried on. Currently, a blue silk blouse over a mini-skirt.

"I thought this was a casual Homecoming dance?" I questioned, looking down at my jeans and t-shirt. "Are you really going to wear silk to a football game? It's supposed to rain tonight."

"Hey, girlfriend, don't go 'disn' on my attempt to bring a little style to this desolate place." She turned around, her hand landing on her hip, as she gave me a once over. "You could at least pretend you're the tiniest bit excited. You've put about as much effort into that outfit as your cousin is putting into her daily appearance these days. Maybe it's in the blood."

"Who, Summer?" I asked.

I hadn't seen either one since our painful afternoon in Seattle. I'd spent the entire time looking over my shoulder, expecting Quentin to appear out of nowhere. But he didn't. And he hasn't. Not since he showed up three weeks ago and sent deafening waves through the quiet at our house. Twenty-one days of Dad's sudden need to know where I'm going and whom I'll be with. Never asking the question he really wants the answer to — but it doesn't matter. I haven't seen him.

"No, the other one," Grace replied as she returned to her closet for another round. "Unless the Rasta look is what she's going for, because that unwashed hair of hers will be dreads soon."

I was trying to picture Autumn on our trip to Seattle. She was quieter than her usual brooding self, but I was so focused on what might be behind me, I couldn't for the life of me remember if she looked more sullen than usual. "When did you see her?"

"How do you not see their beacons of red hair roaming the halls?" She moved back to the mirror and held a black sweater up in front of her. "Too bad you got the watered down version."

I grabbed my watered down mess of kinks and attempted to knot it together on the back of my head. "Well, thanks for that."

"Your strawberry blond locks aren't awful, they're just no match against the ebony goodness," she boasted, swooshing her hand around her black afro.

My hair came cascading down as I pushed myself up off the floor. "Can we please go and get this over with?"

"Girlfriend, you know you're going to enjoy yourself even if it kills you."

"It just might."

CHAPTER
15

"This is not good," Grace said, looking up at the black clouds filling the sky. She pulled her car into the school parking lot, but it was jammed. With nothing else to do in town, every breathing soul had descended on Vashon High in hopes of some Homecoming magic.

"I did mention it was going to rain tonight." I knew I was being a smart-ass, but it felt good to flip a little back her way. She backtracked to the street and worked on her parallel parking skills.

"Damn." Attempt number one failed. "Don't go getting all righteous on me. At least I try to elevate the standards around here." She managed to squeeze into a much larger spot with her second attempt.

I stepped out of the car, inhaling deeply, the cool au-

tumn air tingling through my nose. "We'll see how elevated you feel in that mini-skirt after the game."

She sashayed around the car ending in a catwalk pose. "But, sister, I look good."

I shook my head, unable to engage any further in the inane conversation. We cut across the grass and joined the flow of bodies making their way to the football field in back.

"Do you plan on telling me what's eating at you, or should I try and guess?" she asked. "You've been hovering in funk land for over a month."

"I don't know." I shoved my hands deep in my pockets, unsure of where I would start or how I could possibly explain something I didn't understand. Maybe I should just tell her. Speak it out loud. Test the absurdness on someone else. "I've been having these strange . . ."

"Seriously!" Grace interrupted me once the packed stands came into view. "The good folks of Vashon really need to get a life. How are we expected to find any students?"

I dropped my chin and mouth behind the folds of my scarf, the sharing moment having come and gone. "Text Dylan."

She whipped out her phone, her fingers flying over the buttons. His reply was instantaneous.

"This way," she said before remembering our previous conversation. "What were you saying?"

"Um, nothing," I said over the noise of the crowd as we headed up the south side of the bleachers to where Dylan and Avery were already sitting.

Dylan flagged us down as we got close. "Good thing you two got here when you did," he said, scooting over as I squeezed in next to him.

"These extra bodies are encroaching on our space," Grace snapped, her bare legs already pumping up and down in the cold.

"No kidding." Dylan took notice of the quake Grace was causing to our bench. "Didn't you say African Americans melt in the rain?"

"You. Did. Not!" Grace shot back indignantly. "You did not just call me that. My skin is black, through and through, and I have never once touched a toe to the continent of Africa."

Nonplussed by Grace's outrage, Dylan said, "But you do melt, right?" He glanced down at me and winked. I kept my smirk safely lodged in my scarf.

"Only if directly rained on." Her tone haughty.

"Good thing for you I found seats undercover."

"Yes, it was a good thing."

The crowd erupted onto their feet, stomping and cheering as the Vashon Pirates ran their way onto the field. I was not in a cheerleader kind of mood. My stomach was soured by the realization I was completely alone. In a sea of shivering people gathered under the bright field lights, I was the odd one out. The anomaly.

This was going to be a long game.

"Come on," Avery said as she leaned over and pulled me up. "You better at least pretend like you're cheering them on or you might incite a riot." She rolled her eyes over to Grace who was scanning the field, most likely searching for Sean's number eight jersey.

The game was close. Painfully close, leading to over-time. When it was all said and done, the Pirates were able to squeak by with a Homecoming victory, and we could finally leave.

"Is everyone still going to the dance?" Grace asked through her chattering teeth as we headed down and out of the bleachers.

"No, I want to go home." It wasn't a lie, but the question was stupid. She knew we were all going to the dance. She practically forced it upon us.

"Too bad, since I'm your ride and you will be staying 'til the bitter end."

I pounded my fist to my chest, pained by the torture.

Dylan bent over, his warm breath filling my ear. "Don't worry, Vanderbie. If you want out early, I'll take you home."

I smiled at him, breathing a sigh of relief even though I knew he had ulterior motives. "Thanks."

Righting himself, he raised his voice and said to Grace, "I told Sean we'd meet him in the concession area by the gym."

Grace jumped down off the last step and into the rain, forgetting that she might melt. "He's coming with us?"

I knew this was a surprise to her, the rumor of Chelsey still floating around her thick skull.

"Yeah," he answered, not realizing the impact of the information he'd just delivered. Grace looped her arm through mine, her lightened steps evidence that her mood had been elevated considerably. Maybe it would rub off.

We jostled our way through the bodies exiting the stadium, the atmosphere a mini-stampede. Avery called out from somewhere behind me, "Wait!"

I turned and reached my hand out to her, and I saw him, directly behind Avery. The guy who had been with Evelyn the night of Picasso. Our eyes locked, sending a jolt of electricity through my system. What was his name? Franklin? Fredrick? Felix. Avery grabbed my hand, obscuring my view. I shifted right and scanned the area behind her, but he wasn't there. Nothing. I spun every which way, praying my imagination was not working against me.

"Thanks," Avery panted as she sidled up next to me, grabbing hold of my arm. "I thought I was going to lose you guys."

"We wouldn't ditch ya, girlfriend," Grace chipped as she grabbed her other arm and we broke free from the crowd, my tired body wrestling with my slipping mind.

The concession area outside the gym was packed. Semi-wet students lined up to hand money over to someone's mom so we could step into the gym. A place we

were required to be in every other day of the week. The noise in the small area was grating, fraying my already frazzled nerves.

"Hey, hey, hey," Sean yelled, strutting his way over to us. "Now tell me that wasn't a game."

"Something like that." Grace was downplaying. Obviously so. "Now let's see what kind of stamina you really have. I vote you pass out after the first dance."

"I'll take that bet." He grabbed her hand and bee-lined for the door.

"I guess we're going in now," Dylan noted as we sheep followed suit.

I braced myself for the mayhem I could hear oozing out the door. "So it seems."

We moved in strobe light motion through the gym. The humid air hung heavily, forcing my lungs to work twice as hard. A mass of bodies were already bending and swaying to the high-pitched wails coming from the speakers.

"Come on," Grace yelled after we ditched our coats, motioning to the dance floor.

I was too tired to argue. We followed her and Sean, right into the middle of the ever-shifting amoeba. Dancing. Song after song. The sound waves bouncing off us. Sweat dripped like it was raining inside.

The physical release of the dancing felt freeing, the strobe light flashing like a camera, swaying us in slow motion. I closed my eyes and wallowed in the temporary

relief of the noise. The grating sound filled every crevice inside of me, leaving no room for thought or memory. The light penetrated through my closed eyes. Flash after flash after flash, until they hit.

Tingles.

Painfully surging.

Up my neck.

Over my head.

Releasing a relentless flow of brilliant color before merging into a rerun of frightful images. I spun — my body, my mind — as I tried to catch the racing scene.

It was the dock.

The small wooden boat thrashed in the water, no longer anchored to the shore. A silhouette clung to the edges, trying not to be thrown as the water battered down the sides.

My arms shot out, trying to balance my leaden body through the frenzy of images. The light continued to strobe under my eyelids, turning the scene into a slow motion nightmare while the blaring music taxed my already strained senses.

My stamina was peaking. I worked to shake free from the images, but darkness surged in and dropped me to the ground. Toes and heels were everywhere. Kicking. Jabbing. Inflicting unabating pain up the side of my body.

Unable to lift myself up, I curled my body in on itself, crossing my arms tightly over my face. Time stretched on, unstoppable, before I felt hands grab hold of me and

pull me up from the darkness. Dylan and Sean stood on either side, holding me steady.

"What happened? Are you okay?" Dylan asked, puzzlement ringing in his voice as he shouted above the music.

"I slipped," I choked out, trying to contain the pain and fear building inside of me.

"Do you want to sit one out?" Grace asked, but I knew she didn't want to relinquish her time on the dance floor with Sean.

"Or do you want to go home?" Dylan blessedly asked.

"Yes. Please. Will you take me home?" I held tight to the dam that threatened to break inside me. It happened. Again. And he wasn't here.

"Sure."

I walked out of the gym as normally as possible. Searing pain shot up my legs and lower back, screaming out — reminding me of just how normal I wasn't.

"Wait," Grace yelled, running after us. I turned and waited. "You're really leaving? Are you sure? Do you want me to drive you home?"

"Don't worry about it," my strained voice tried to assure her. I could tell by the look in her eye she was suspicious, but Sean waiting for her to return was working in my favor. "I'm just tired. Enjoy. I'll call you in the morning."

She bent over and hugged me, the squeeze inflaming my bruised body.

We quietly walked through the rain to Dylan's old Honda before he asked, "Tired?"

I carefully lowered myself into the passenger seat. "Yeah, I guess."

I was in no mood for small-talk. I watched the night pass outside my window, trying to keep my fear at bay. It happened. Again. And without Quentin. It was me. All me. Quentin had nothing to do with it, other than being subjected to my freakishness.

I couldn't think about it. Not now.

"Any other plans for the weekend?" Dylan tried to ask casually. The air shifted, like the nervous energy of some-one trying to add electricity to the current.

"Not much." I leaned my head against the cool glass. "Homework and stuff."

He turned his car into my driveway and stopped near the garage, the engine idling, waiting for one of us to make a move. I reached for the handle and opened the door. The harshness of the overhead light cast a gloomy yellow hue over us, highlighting the indecision playing out on his face. "Good night," I said, stepping out into the heavy rain coming down, making the decision for him.

"Good night," he replied, hesitation still lingering. "I hope you're not too bruised from your fall."

The bruises were the least of my worries. "Bruises heal." I closed the door and walked into the house, not looking back.

CHAPTER
16

The house was tranquil. A glow of light spilled from the kitchen door, producing swathes of shadows that reached out and clung tightly to the furniture, trying to pull them out of darkness. I shrugged out of my wet coat, hanging it next to the key rack by the front door. Gingerly, I followed the lure of light to where my dad still sat awake behind his computer.

I cautiously stepped into the room and glanced at the kitchen clock. Eleven thirty-seven. "I didn't think you'd be up."

"I was paying bills." His computer nicely read him the information he needed to know. "As a matter of fact, I was going over your cell phone bill."

The uptake was slow, but my heart dropped with the pit that landed deep in my stomach.

"It seems there's a new number you've been calling and texting over the past month. I would ask you to tell me who it is, but I called the number myself."

"You called the number?" I spat out, shocked. Anger boiled up painfully in my body. "You had no right . . ."

"I have every right," his raised voiced cut me off. "You lied to me. You both lied to me."

"I can't believe you called him. I haven't talked to him since the day he came to the house. He probably thinks I'm some prudish freak having my dad call his cell phone."

"I only got his voice mail, but it doesn't matter. You have a lot of explaining to do."

"No. I. Don't," I yelled back, unable to stop my pain and frustration from spewing out. "It doesn't work this way. You can't just decide you're going to start butting into my life after being an absentee father since Mom died."

"And you can't run around with older guys behind my back." He stood up, bracing himself on the table, his eyes unable to find me. "Especially ones you know nothing about. Something's not right about him."

"Not right about him? Are you kidding? Not right. About. HIM! You have no idea what I know and don't know," I countered furiously. "You don't know him. You don't know me. And you sure as hell don't deserve to . . ."

I couldn't finish. I was pissed. I stomped from the kitchen, fury igniting with every painful step across the

living room. Without thought, I grabbed my car keys off the key rack and ran into the rain — away from my dad. Away from the painful life he represented. I revved my car to life and tore out of the driveway. Aimlessly I drove, up one street and down another, barely seeing through my tears and the constant fog that covered the front windshield.

How dare he play Dad after abandoning Foster and me, leaving us to drown in our own pain. Alone, scared, with no assurances that a new day would rise. Mom would never have done that to us, no matter the circumstances. She would never have lied to us about her own family.

No longer able to see through the thick fog on the windshield, I pulled my car into the ferry commuter lot. As I reached in the back to feel around for a rag to wipe the windows, the horn of the approaching ferry startling me. I gave up the search and leaned my head on the headrest. The horn blared again, inflaming the spaces of aggravation in my mind.

The sound of cars unloading caught my attention, and before I could formulate a plan, I jumped out of my car and ran through the rain to the waiting ferry. A haven. Something to carry me away from this god-forsaken place.

I stepped aboard and walked heavily up the stairs, keeping my tear-swollen eyes pointed down. I bee-lined straight to the bathroom. Disinfectant cleaner swirled

sharply through my nose, jarring me as I caught sight of myself in the mirror. A painful reflection of the truth, calling me out for what I was. A freak. A freak with wet, limp hair, and streaks of black eyeliner, preparing me for a part in the side-show.

"That's me," I muttered. "The freak in the side-show."

Out of nowhere, *Que Sera Sera* began to spin its melody through my head, the same way my mom used to hum it as she worked . . . *the future's not ours to see* . . . The tinkling sounds of the piano reminded me of caramel covered apples and carousel rides. But my head bent the notes. Warped them. Distorted them. Forcing the carousel to spin off-kilter with no intention of ever stopping.

I pushed on the faucet, cupped my hands under the sputtering spray, and prayed the cold water would shake away the pain of the warped song. Of the night. That the splash would wash away the disappointed look that hung from Dad's face before I ran out.

I grabbed a wad of paper towels and wiped the eyeliner off my cheeks, the dock reflecting back in my eyes. The little boat. Someone clinging for dear life in the night.

I shook it off. Panic building. Walls caving. I wanted to give into the exhaustion seeping into my arms and legs, to shut down and curl up on the cold, smelly bathroom tiles and end my own private torture, but the horn blasted, forcing me to move. It was a slow, painful movement from the bathroom to the front of the boat.

With my head down, I wrapped my arms tight across my chest and clamped my teeth together to keep them from clattering as I made my way to where the passenger bridge was being lowered into place.

A bridge leading to no one.

To nothing.

To nowhere.

I followed the path of least resistance and moved with a small group of people crossing through the terminal and out to the breezeway. But the group quickly disbanded, leaving me to forge my own path.

Avoiding the massive downpour, I turned west and descended under the viaduct, an eye-sore that blemished the entire downtown shoreline.

The damp air seeped under my skin, sending quakes of chills through my body. My nerves worked feverishly to keep surveillance on my surroundings. Every ounce of flesh stood at attention, questioning the wisdom of my swift decision to travel Seattle by foot, without a coat, without a purse, without a phone.

A small group of people popped out of a dark alley, our paths nearly colliding. My heart lurched into my throat stopping the air from escaping, tumbling me anxiously as they moved on, laughing, oblivious of my presence.

I backed up against a brick wall. My breath stilted. What was I doing?

Tears rolled down my cheeks. I needed to bolt, to get

back on the ferry, but the lack of motion caused my legs to buckle and I slowly slid down the wall, my descent unstoppable. As were the harsh tingles and ravaging images that once again took control of my body.

The dock.

The boat.

The thrashing water threatening to topple the shadowy figure that clung desperately to the sides.

I tried to push them back, to gain control of my mind and move my legs back underneath me, but the resistance in my head caused my decision making to lag.

Open your eyes and stand, I told myself, refusing to pass out in the dark. Alone. *Open your eyes and stand.*

I forced my eyes open and focused all my energy to my legs, using the wall to brace my punishing progress. I had to find a phone. A way out of here.

I looked around the dark viaduct, my eyes locking onto the glow of a small neon sign.

OK Hotel.

My eyes focused on the "OK," my painful gait praying it would be as I limped toward the door where a large man dressed in black was checking ID.

"You're not twenty-one," he said brusquely.

"I know. I just need to borrow a phone"

"You need to be twenty-one."

Desperate pleas tumbled from my mouth. "I'm stranded and really need to call a friend to pick me up."

"You can't go in the club," he said, eyeing me suspiciously. After a lifetime of seconds, he reached in his pocket and pulled out a cell phone. "You'll stand right there. You have one minute."

I had to keep myself from throwing my arms around him in relief. "Thank you."

I turned my back and dialed his number. The rings were endless until his voicemail kicked in. I couldn't believe it. "Quentin. It's Cee. I'm down near the OK Hotel and could really use a ride." I hung up, hating the sound of my helpless and pathetic voice.

I handed the phone back to the bouncer. "Thanks."

"Friend on the way?"

"Um, yeah. Should be here soon," I lied, moving my exhausted body away from the door. Away from yet another person looking at me like I was a freak.

I wandered in and out of the parked cars that stretched on as far as the eye could see, the muffled ferry horn blowing in the distance. I couldn't go back. I had no money. No nothing. I had no idea where to go. Minutes stretched forever.

"Miss? Are you okay?" I heard a male voice ask, but assumed he was talking to someone else.

I continued to weave in and out of the cars.

The voice grew closer. "Miss? Do you need help? Have you lost your car?"

I turned around. A guy in his mid-thirties, dressed in khaki's and a blazer was pointing at me, closing the gap

between us. The dark reared up, causing a fine layer of sweat to break out over my freezing body. "Um, no. I'm fine."

"I can help."

"I don't need help," I said, trying not to be crippled by the frenzy of fear inside me.

"Everyone needs a little help now and then." He moved closer. Close enough to pinch down on my shoulder. I instinctively came out swinging, and backhanded him across the face. He shook off the sting and gripped my arm like a vice.

"You shouldn't have done that," he hissed. The stench of his alcohol laced breath set off my gag reflex.

"She's with me."

I turned as Quentin stepped from the shadows, his dark clothes blending perfectly with the night. My body flooded with relief at the sound of his commanding voice, while my eyes drank in his beautiful, severe features.

"I think this one can talk for herself," the man said indignantly, letting go of my arm with a push. My bruised legs collapsed under me. "And I believe she's with me."

Quentin's reply came in the form of a right hook to the man's jaw line, followed by a left one to the gut.

The guy doubled over writhing in pain.

"Hey!" someone behind me yelled, stirring up a commotion in the parking lot.

Before I could grasp what was happening, Quentin squatted down and scooped me up, moving us away from the small gathering of night owls.

I twisted my head over Quentin's shoulder and watched the man stand and stumble. His confused features had replaced the bravado of his masculine prowess. "Quentin, shouldn't we call the police or . . ." I began to ask.

"Hold still." His tone was harsh in my ear, which my body responded to and froze. I clung to his black coat, shivering. Greedily inhaling his musky scent. The man's shouts becoming a distant tirade.

My body relaxed into his as he carried me to his car and deposited me down on the passenger seat. He slammed the door closed, jarring my senses.

He silently climbed in and turned over the engine, tearing out of the parking lot and into the rain.

"What happened . . . back . . . there?" I whispered in the dark car, my shivers impeding my ability to talk coherently. "I don't understand why . . . How did you get here so fast?"

Quentin cranked the heater full blast. "How about we not play twenty questions." His voice was curt, his face fierce with anger.

I sat, quietly, not having the energy to fight. He sped north on Alaskan Way and made his way into the heart of Queen Anne, the Space Needle loomed over us as we passed the Seattle Center. We zig-zagged up one street and down another. I was completely disoriented.

Abruptly, he pulled his car into a driveway with a small white house that sat back from the road. Every

window was pitch black. Not even a porch light hinted that someone lived here. Without a word, he got out and made the reverse trek back to my door. He opened it and stood perfectly still. I did the same because I didn't think I could stand without falling.

"Are you coming in?"

Determined not to feel intimidated by his scowl, I stared straight ahead and said, "I can't."

He exhaled sharply. "CeeCee, get out of the car." He paused and added, "Please."

I gingerly swung my legs around without looking at him and placed both feet firmly on the ground, attempting to stand. As I shifted the balance of my weight, my legs crumpled. I waited for the fall. But it didn't come. Instead, I was cradled back in Quentin's arms as he carried me out of the black of night and into the shadows of his home.

My eyes were slow to adjust, peeking over his shoulder, trying to get my bearings. He pulled me away from his chest, my body hovering in thin air before he gently set me down on a cool, leather couch and disappeared into the darkness. I strained to hear him as he moved about, opening and closing doors. And then all was silent. Too silent. Until something draped around me, causing me to jump and send a painful jolt through my bruised body.

A small table lamp flicked on. I squinted against the soft glow, waiting for my pupils to adjust. Quentin

reached out and pulled the blanket tight around my shivering body and sat down next to me, his nearness wreaking a havoc all its own.

"You need to get in a hot shower." His face was expressionless. His perfected barrier in place.

"It happened again." The words just popped out. I couldn't look at him. Instead my eyes darted around the bare room. There were no pictures or art, hardly anything to fill the space contained by the four walls. "Out of nowhere. It happened again. Without you. You weren't there."

He took a deep breath and ran both hands through his hair. "Where were you?"

"At school. A dance. I fell. I couldn't get up. I couldn't get out from underneath the trampling feet." His hand moved to my lower back where I'd been kicked. Reflexively I pulled away, his touch sending a jolt of pain through my body.

Misunderstanding my movement, he quickly snatched his hand back, his voice frustrated. "What did you see?"

The images tumbled urgently from my mouth. "It was the boat again. And someone was in it. Clinging desperately to the sides. Water was everywhere."

He sat up straighter. "Was it any clearer?"

"No. But it was desperate. It felt desperate." I felt desperate.

"If you were at a dance, how did you end up at the OK Hotel?" The hardness in his voice was back.

My eyes quickly danced over his face before looking away. "I fought with my dad and ran out."

A huge breath whooshed from his mouth. "Do you want to talk about it?"

My flight from the island suddenly felt childish under his scrutiny. "No," I said quietly, a tear escaping from my neatly contained dam. "It doesn't matter."

He reached out, cupped his hand to the side of my face as his thumb brushed away the tear. The hurt. The fear.

I turned, my eyes traveling to find his. The deep cuts of his face turned vulnerable, the softness catching me off guard. Without thought, I shook my arm free from the blanket and carefully reached out, tracing the soft line of his scar with the tips of my fingers.

Overwhelmed with emotion, I leaned in. Hovering. Waiting. Unsure.

Until I saw it.

A warm smolder in his eyes as he laced his fingers in my hair, pulling me to him, closing the gap, sealing his lips over mine. He pulled me tighter, the new sensation over-riding the pain shooting through me, creating a new energy all its own. Energy that escalated with every breath we tried to catch. It was electrifying, without thought, without care. Unburdened by the outside world.

Abruptly he stood, pushing away from me.

"This can't happen. You have no idea," he said through clenched teeth. He stormed from the room, leaving me

alone to stumble and catch my breath. I touched my lips, still warm from his. When he returned, he held out a chocolate brown towel to me. "You need to take a shower before your shivering turns into hypothermia."

I needed to leave and save a shred of my rejected dignity. "I need to catch a ferry."

"It's after two in the morning. The ferries have quit running."

Painfully I stood, determined not to be the one left broken on the couch. I was tired. Tired of people telling me what to do. Telling me what I knew and what I didn't know. Bravely, I asked, "Why did you come for me? How did you get there so fast? Why didn't we call the cops?"

"The guy was drunk. I was not about to waste time on statements, only for him to get a slap on the wrist and walk." His answer was quick. Too quick. He began pacing.

I stood and pressed on. "Quentin, how did you find me so fast?"

"I was already downtown when you called." He stopped and focused his intimidating eyes on me, the returned lines cutting severe paths across his face. "You shouldn't have been anywhere near there."

His answer brought me up short. I took in his dark clothes, realization dawning that he'd probably been out on a date. One I interrupted and then topped off by throwing myself at him. The thought was mortifying. I imagine the heat in my cheeks would be obvious to that.

Interrupting my thoughts, he said with a sigh, "CeeCee, it's been a long night. I think you should take a hot shower and crash."

Too fatigued to argue anymore, I snatched the towel out of his hand and shuffled my feet along the hardwood floors to the bathroom. It was as bare as the living room. The only sign of use was a rumpled hand towel and a toothbrush lying on the counter.

I locked the door and bypassed the truth of the mirror. I pushed in the plug and filled the tub with scalding hot water. The rising steam soothing as I gingerly peeled off my clothes and slid down into the enveloping warmth.

My eyes followed the jagged lines of the tiles, the surreal evening sinking in. The weight of exhaustion pulled me down further, along with the last of my shivers, which dissolved in the heat of the water. I remained perfectly still, my ears floating underwater, heightening my silent isolation.

Slow to rise out of the tepid water, I stepped out and wrapped the large bath towel around me, my loose hair dripping down my back. I bent over and pulled the plug. The sucking sound of the escaping water flooded my senses and overloaded my body with tingles and vibrant color. It was all back.

The boat.

The storm.

The shadow.

The fear.

The painful needle penetration gripping my entire head.

I slipped to the ground, willing the face to be clear. "Who are you?" I whispered in frustration. "Show me your face."

The scene was suddenly flooded in brilliance and she turned, her red hair whipping wildly in the wind. The fear of death painted on Autumn's face.

"NO!" A blood-curdling scream escaped my lips. I reached out. Tried to touch her. Tried to grasp hold of her, but the shadows converged, stealing her away, leaving only a vortex of darkness.

I forced my eyes open, but the room remained dark. I closed and open my eyes again. Nothing. Nothing but black. My hands reached out. Touching. Feeling. Trying to make my way to the light switch.

The rap on the door startled me. "CeeCee? Are you okay?"

I couldn't find the light switch. I couldn't see my hand. My fingers. Nothing but darkness filled my eyes and senses. I was slipping into a void, grasping to stay conscious.

"Cee?" The anxiousness of Quentin's voice seeped under the door, unable to retract the darkness caving in. The locked doorknob jiggled. "CeeCee, open the door!"

I grabbed tight to my towel and tried to move, the excruciating pain in my body brutishly overthrowing my efforts. I couldn't see. I opened and closed my eyes as quick as I could. Nothing. I couldn't see.

"I can't see!" My panic turned audible and the screams flew from my mouth. "I can't see! I can't fucking see! I have to find her. You have to help me find Autumn!"

The sound of ripping wood cracked through the small bathroom, billowing cold air over the humid space, waving up the scent of Quentin as he knelt next to me. "What happened?"

"I can't see!" I screamed again, squeezing my eyes shut.

He grabbed either side of my face, the nearness of him intensifying my desperation. "Open your eyes and look at me," he commanded.

Unquestioning, I opened my eyes, fully expecting to see his face hovering over mine. There was nothing. Terror was taking hold. I tried to push him away. "I can't see. There's nothing. Nothing. Nothing. I can't see anything."

He pinned my arms to my side, his frighteningly calm voice ordering, "CeeCee, just open your eyes and look at me."

"I told you . . ."

He didn't wait for me to finish. "Look at me. You have to look at me. Just open your eyes and look at me."

The first shifts were miniscule. I couldn't even be certain of them. Then, like clouds dissipating after a dark thunderous storm, the shadows gradually slipped away like ghosts, revealing Quentin's tempestuous face in front of mine.

My arms shot out and clung to his neck. He scooped me up and carried me down the hall, every fear, every

ounce of horror, every unsettling event, flowed out of my eyes, leaving pools of water on Quentin's shirt.

He shouldered open a door and crossed the room, gently laying me on his bed. I couldn't let go of his neck. My arms wouldn't budge, terrified of being left alone with myself.

"What's happening to me?" I sobbed into his neck. "I couldn't see. I was fine until I saw . . ." It hit like a freight train — Autumn, fighting to stay alive in the boat.

My body lurched, pulling away from Quentin. "It's Autumn." The alarm of my voice rang clearly in the room. "I need a phone! I saw her! SHE'S IN THE BOAT!"

"CeeCee, what the hell . . ." he whooshed, running his hand over the bruises that made a knarly trail up my thigh. "What happened to your leg?"

"Phone!" I screamed in near hysteria. "I need a phone!"

He marched out of the room, returning with his cell phone in hand.

I quickly dialed Aunt Lucy's house. Uncle Russell picked up after only one ring. "Hello?"

"Uncle Russell. It's CeeCee."

"CeeCee! Where are you?" I could hear relief in his voice.

"It doesn't matter, where's Autumn?"

"We don't know. We hoped she was with you."

My hesitation was a half of heartbeat, knowing demands for answers would await me. My eyes locked on

Quentin's as I replied, "You need to go to the lighthouse. Someone needs to get down to Old Robinson Lighthouse and look for her out on the water."

"CeeCee, there's a storm going on," his voice registering fear. "Why would she be . . .?"

"GO!" I yelled. "You have to go now!"

Without a further word, the line went dead and I fell back on the bed, covering my face with my arm as another flood of tears rushed out. Quentin stood up and pulled the comforter around me.

"Who's Autumn?" he asked quietly, the bed bending under his weight as he sat back down. Gently he began to stroke the back of my head.

"Cousin," I managed to say between sobs. His fingers were soothing on my scalp. Methodical. Slowly pushing up before gently stroking back down.

"Why was she on the boat?"

"I don't know," I choked out. "I don't know if she was . . . is . . . was . . ."

"How did you know she was out there?" The hesitant tone of his voice was not lost on me, but all energy to deal with it was gone.

"I have no . . . idea." My mind was spinning down a vortex of exhaustion, slowly slipping from my grasp.

Up went his fingers.

And Down.

Up.

Down.

I rolled over, pulling the comforter tight around me, and curled my head in his lap. The overwhelming relief of finally seeing Autumn's face and the fatigue of unburdening the information took hold, luring my broken body to sleep.

CHAPTER
18

I lingered in a fitful state of darkness. The circuit board in my head fired intermittently, sending inklings of something that lay unresolved. I willed myself to return to the murky recesses of my mind, but light seeped through the slits of my eyes and foiled my attempts to hold tight to unconsciousness.

Heavy with sleep, I pushed my resistant lids open.

My nose was sunk deep in a pillow coated with a familiar smell. I lifted my head high enough to read the red numbers on the clock. Nine twenty-one. Red numbers. Red numbers? As soon as the realization hit that the numbers on my own alarm clock were green, the floodgates opened, unleashing every moment, every disturbing memory of the past twenty-four hours.

The dance.

The fight.

The rain.

The parking lot.

Quentin.

The images.

Autumn.

Autumn clinging for dear life as I fought to see through the darkness I'd become trapped in. That is, until Quentin somehow shook me free from the brink of a complete mental collapse.

Determined to stop the instant replay in my head, I sat up, every ache and bruise screaming louder than the memories churning in my head.

But I could see.

My sight was as clear as it ever was. I glanced around Quentin's meagerly furnished bedroom, his minimalist décor in keeping with the rest of the house. A bare, tall highboy dresser held up the far wall, while a small night table with a clock and lamp sat next to the queen bed. I was tempted to open the closet door to see if there were actual clothes inside it, but decided to search out the elusive resident of the house. And a phone.

My stomach churned at the thought of calling home. I needed to know, to hear for myself Autumn had been found, and that she was safe, but I was unsure if I had the strength to take on the barrage of questions the call

would bring. I had no answers, no explanation for how I knew where Autumn was, and no answers would undoubtedly lead to another ugly fight.

The comforter fell away as I swung my legs out from underneath it, revealing a guy's over-sized t-shirt hanging on my body. My cheeks burned, unable to remember how or when the shirt replaced the towel I'd been wrapped in. I stood and moved delicately to the partially open door leading from the room. Nudging it open wider, I peered up and down the hallway. There was no sound, no movement, but I didn't let the quiet fool me.

With one hand balanced on the wall, I walked vigilantly down the hall. My sore legs were like burdensome children, fighting each step, threatening to topple me over. The living room felt even more barren in the harsh light of day, except for the breathtaking view of the Puget Sound that shimmered through the glass of the large picture window.

The dark clouds of the night had lifted, leaving a mild gray day hovering over the water. I stood and stared out at a small sailboat gently listing back and forth, waiting patiently for the wind to fill its sails.

I turned back to the room, unsure of what to do, hesitant to call out and be the only voice echoing off the walls. I slipped carefully across the room and rounded a corner into the kitchen. Bright white counter tiles glistened back at me, devoid of any clutter, including a phone. Maybe he just moved in.

Intending to move back to the living room, I noticed another door with a bolt lock near the back of the kitchen. I shuffled across the cold floor and glanced over my shoulder, expecting Quentin to appear from where ever he was hidden. My heart thumped against my ribs as I tested the knob and pulled the door open, revealing a staircase.

"Quentin?" I called down. The sound of my voice unnatural against the quiet.

Nothing.

"Quentin?" I called again and held my breath so I could hear over the throbbing pulse whooshing through my ears.

Nothing. Only silence.

I felt along the wall for a light switch, but found none. With one last glance over my shoulder, I squeezed through the door and stepped down onto the top stair. A hair-raising squeak reverberated in the stairwell, alerting the entire house that someone was on the move. I waited. Held my breath. Counted backward from thirty.

And still the silence droned on.

Throwing rational thought to the wind, I quickly descended the rest of the stairs, trying to minimize the moans and groans of the old house.

I stepped tentatively into the musty basement, the unfinished walls polished in dust and cobwebs. The chill of the cement floor radiated through my bare feet and up my legs like ivy, releasing a layer of goose bumps across

my skin. My eyes dilated wide, the faint lines of a washer and dryer coming into focus on the far wall. And a door.

Another door.

My feet moved forward without a command from me, every muscle in my body strained tight. I turned the knob. The door pushed open. I stood perfectly still, staring into the black abyss. Politeness told me to leave and return upstairs, but instead, I curled my hand around the door jam, walked my fingers over a light plate, and pushed up the switch.

The bare single bulb dangling from the unfinished ceiling revealed a stark row of faces staring back at me. Photos, hanging on a line running the length of the room, displayed slices of humanity secretly captured — the young and the old, the beautiful and the ugly. I slid past each one, their presence compelling, haunting, leaving me yearning to know more. But it was the last one that stopped me cold and stole by breath.

It was me. My face. Perfectly framed between the brush growing up from the ground and a tree bending precariously with the contours of my body. Nothing in my expression registered the looming threat hanging over me. My only expression was peace, contently washed over my face. I tried to recreate our walk through the woods to the lighthouse, but no memory shook free of him pointing his camera in my direction and capturing a slice of a moment I couldn't remember.

A shiver ran down my spine, the cold of the basement infiltrating my bare arms and legs. I backed up, my foot catching on something. My arm shot to the wall to steady my balance as I glanced down at the corner of a tarp my toes had become ensnared in. I reached down to untangle myself, a glint of gold catching my eye as the tarp shifted out of place. Curious, I lifted the corner and peaked underneath, spying a frame. I lifted it further, until I'd uncovered seven different works of art beautifully framed. Oils and acrylics, just sitting and rotting in the damp basement. I didn't get it. Why wouldn't he take the time to hang them up?

I dropped the canvas back in place and turned to inspect the rest of the room. On the opposite side was a light table next to a desk covered in computer monitors and a keyboard. Tacked on the wall above the desk was a map of Seattle and outlying areas dotted with small pins tipped in yellow and red.

I crept closer. The pattern was random, marching in swirls that made no sense. Embedded amongst the red and yellow, were two dots of black hiding, hardly distinguishable in the mess of color. One marked an address at the top of Queen Anne, while the other was pushed directly into my address on Vashon Island. I was taken back, unsure of what to make of it.

I bit down on my lip and slowly reached up and pulled out the pin, a gaping hole now indicating where

my house should be. I stared at the hole, confused. Why would he . . .?

My lower lip throbbed, my teeth still painfully embedded in the flesh. Releasing my caught lip, the blood flow began to beat in time with the questions swirling through me. My dad's voice adding to the chaos, *"Something's not right about him."*

"What are you doing down here?"

I startled at the sound of Quentin's dark voice, his statuesque body filling the doorway. How did I not hear him come down the stairs?

"Quentin," I breathed out, catching my startled breath. "You shouldn't sneak up on people."

"This is my house. It's not considered sneaking." He stepped into the room holding a drink carrier with four latte cups. His hard eyes scanned the area around his computer. "You're the one sneaking around."

"Sorry, um, you're right," I acknowledged, knowing I had no excuse. I gave the pin a discrete toss under the desk and moved away from the map, hoping he wouldn't notice the hole. "I was looking for a phone."

"There isn't one down here."

"So I noticed." I pointed to the drink carrier he was holding in hopes of a distraction. "Do you always drink four cups of coffee in the morning?"

'No." He moved back to the door, waiting for me walk through first. "I didn't know what you wanted."

I stopped in the doorframe, the scent of him blending with the bitter bean aroma. "What are my choices?"

"Latte. Chai. Mocha."

"I'll take the Chai."

I circled my fingers around the warm cup he handed me and stepped from the room, unable to reconcile the inconsistent pictures of Quentin in my head.

I scooted up the stairs, self-conscious of my bare legs sticking out of his t-shirt, which suddenly felt much shorter as he trailed a step behind me.

His thoughts weren't too far from mine. "What happened to your leg?"

I glanced down at my leg as I stepped through the door at the top of the stairs. A trail of bruises twisted down my thigh. "I fell and got kicked."

"When?" he asked, his warm eyes roaming over my leg.

"At the dance. I fell when, um . . . I saw . . ." I stuttered as his eyes traveled up my body to mine, releasing a wave of heat in my chest. I broke the contact and moved to the other side of the kitchen. "Um, well, it's nothing. I need to get dressed."

"Your clothes are in the bathroom." He closed the door firmly and turned the key bolt above the knob. "They should be dry. I'll drive you home after you get dressed."

He slid the key into his pocket, his eyes catching mine before I turned and stepped anxiously from the room.

I didn't understand what warranted being locked in the musty basement, especially since he took such little care with his art.

"My car is parked on the other side, you can just drop me off at the ferry terminal."

"I told your Dad I would drive you home."

I whipped around. "You talked to my dad?" I asked incredulously. "When? Why would you do that?"

"I called him last night after you fell asleep. He deserved to know you were alive." He moved around me, not actually looking at me. "By the way, they found your cousin."

"Alive?"

"Yes."

"Was she in the boat?"

"Yes." He came to a stop in front of the large picture window, his back highlighted by the light filtering through. "But you knew that already."

It was an accusation, one I didn't have a reply to. "Did my dad ask how I knew where she was?"

"No."

"About how I ended up here?"

"No."

Of course he didn't. Concern took effort and effort he didn't expend. I took my frustration out on the easy target in front of me. "Are we going to talk about last night? The guy in the parking lot? My temporary loss of sight?

Autumn?" I didn't bother adding the kiss to the list.

His "no" came out forcefully. "There's nothing to talk about. You should get dressed."

I was done. Fed up with his evasiveness. It was obvious he wanted me gone. My feet stomped from the room, my mouth muttering my thoughts out loud, "Coward."

In two loud strides he caught up to me and grabbed hold my arm, spinning me around to face the indignation etched deep on his face. "What did you call me?"

"Coward. I called you a coward," I snapped, pulling my arm from his grip, my Chai latte erupting over my hand. I was too mad to back down from the anger his face radiated like a red flag. "Is this how you treat everyone who crosses your threshold?"

"Nobody comes here."

"Well, it's no wonder." Tired of his insolent tone, I pulled myself tall, unable to stop my stream of consciousness from exiting my mouth. "You can pretend like I'm the one losing it, but it's a lie. We both know it. I. Am. Not. Crazy."

"What do you want from me? I didn't ask for this."

"Then why did you kiss me?"

"I didn't. You kissed me."

"Oh, that's right, your lips didn't participate." My voice dripped in sarcasm.

"It shouldn't have happened. None of it. And it wouldn't have if you had been less impulsive and not

jumped ship to leave the island."

"Is this how life is for you? Hiding in this empty house, insulting anyone within earshot, heaping your oh-so-worthy opinions on them?" I spit out, waving my arms around the bare room. "Because it's painfully obvious that you enjoy avoiding everything else."

I spun and headed down the hall. His dark voice barreled down at me as I marched toward the bathroom to change. "Don't pretend like you know me. You know nothing about me."

I stepped into the bathroom and turned, bracing myself between the door and the shredded doorframe. Suddenly, his harsh features no longer felt threatening. I could see them for what they were — a simple ruse to keep everyone at bay. "That, Quentin, is completely by choice." And I slammed the bathroom door closed.

CHAPTER
19

The ride was quiet. Agonizingly quiet. But I refused to relent. I sat perfectly still, my eyes never wavering from the front windshield.

Quentin slammed out of the silent car once we boarded the ferry and didn't return until we had to move off the boat. I didn't bother to give him directions to the house. He knew where I lived — the gapping hole left in his map was proof of that.

We pulled into the driveway and parked next to my aunt's car.

"Great," I mumbled under my breath as I pushed opened the door, my feet crunching down on the gravel. I was barely prepared to answer Dad's questions, let alone my aunt's. My hand was poised to close the door when

I looked across the seats and saw Quentin getting out. "What are you doing?"

He stood on the opposite side, looking back through the car. "I'm coming with you."

My eyes grew wide in disbelief. "Oh, no you're not."

He didn't bother to reply. Instead, he closed his door and headed toward the house. I slammed mine shut and hustled as fast as my aching legs would move. "I didn't ask you to come in," I called out to his unrelenting backside.

"I wasn't waiting for an invitation."

"Is this about the coward comment?" I leapt up onto the porch, squeezing myself between him and the door. "Because now is not a good time to prove otherwise. I can barely handle what is waiting on the other side of the door, let alone trying to defend you."

"This may come as a shock, CeeCee, but I've managed to take care of and fend for myself for nineteen years." His eyes smoldered. "Without your help."

"Well, you didn't do a very good job," I shot back, pointing to the long scar that now seemed as much a part of his features as his nose and mouth. He flinched but held his ground.

I was being unfair, I knew it, but I was anxious, embarrassed. I didn't want him to see that while our house was filled with furniture and art, it was as empty as his.

He leaned forward, his breath warm on my face, his hard features appearing anything but fearsome. The pause

that lingered set off a swarm of electricity inside me, buzzing down to my fingers and toes. His arm reached around me and I waited. Prepared for the pressure on my back, one that would pull me to him. My eyes began to drift close when I heard him knock on the door.

My eyes flew back open, draining the buzz of electricity into the air, Quentin's eyes twinkling with smugness. I spun around and turned the handle, shoving the door open.

"CeeCee?" My dad rose quickly from the couch, dropping his cane, stumbling toward me. I caught his outstretched hands, working to hold him steady and balance us both in the unprecedented gesture. He pulled his hands from mine and tightly wrapped his arms around me. The squeeze welled up tears of pain and unexpected emotions. I bit my lip hard, holding back a cry that threatened to escape my lips.

"Dad, I'm okay," I muttered into his chest, trying to catch my breath.

He stepped back and clamped his hands on either side of my face, his forehead resting on mine. "Never again. Promise me you will not run off ever again. I can't lose you, too."

My eyes dropped to the ground, unable to hold the intense emotion on Dad's face. "I'm sorry, Dad," I whispered, forgetting for a moment that anyone else was standing in the room. Forgetting that my anger had left Dad wondering if he had lost someone else.

My dad righted himself, keeping one arm wrapped tightly around my shoulders. "Quentin?"

"Yes, sir?" he replied politely, taking a step closer.

Dad stretched his free hand in the direction of Quentin's voice. "Thank you."

Quentin closed the gap and shook his hand, his smug eyes finding mine, no hint of cowardice lurking in them. "You're welcome."

"This little family reunion is very sweet, but we have more pressing matters to discuss." We all turned to Aunt Lucy, who was standing stiffly in front of the fireplace.

"Lucy, this is not the time or place," Dad's tone signaling a conversation was not going to happen. "We will resolve what we need to resolve later, after CeeCee has rested."

"Dad, it's okay." I needed to hear that Autumn was going to be fine. "How is she?"

"Autumn? Quietly impetuous with a broken arm, but she'll mend." Her reply was callous. I hadn't realized the toll Autumn's disappearance would have on her. "Although, it seems you are too, aren't you?"

"I'm sorry," I said guiltily, wishing the images in my mind had been clearer. Had come sooner.

"When did they start CeeCee?"

My body stiffened at the exact moment Dad's did, his arm tightening around my shoulder. What was she asking? My eyes found Quentin's, but before I could think of what to say, my dad interjected. A new edge to his

voice sliced through the room. "I said this was not the time, Lucy. This is my house and you will respect my wishes."

"Respect? Is this how you teach your children respect, by letting them lie to you? Keep secrets from you? Although, you've set a fine example for secret keeping." She shifted her icy stare back to me. I hardly recognized her. "Are you going to tell your father when your visions started? Or should I get the ball rolling?"

"How do you know . . .?"

"Because you're not special, you're not unique, you're not the first to have them." She pointed her finger at Quentin. "Is he the one who was with you?"

"Yes . . .no . . .Who else has them?" I stammered, overwhelmed by the notion that someone beside myself had walked this dark path before.

"Your grandmother for one," she spit out, taking a threatening step forward. "Did you mention to your father that you met her, or did you keep that little secret to yourself too?"

Out of the corner of my eye, I saw Quentin shift. His movement subtle, placing his body partially between my aunt and me. The scene unfolding was unreal. "How do you know . . .?"

"Because she told me. Who do you think would set up something as extravagant as the Picasso evening in the first place?"

Holding me tight, my dad gulped down his surprise and lied to his sister. "Of course she told me about meeting her."

"Did she tell you that Mother and, and, that boy," she stuttered, thrusting a finger in Quentin's direction, "were both present for what appears to have been her initial release?"

"Initial, what?" Frustration wrung my body inside out. "I passed out. Nothing else. The fact that Quentin happened to be there was a fluke."

"It was not a *fluke,* CeeCee. There are no such things as coincidences in this family. Everything has a purpose, including him." She pointed again to Quentin like he was a piece of furniture to be sat on. "He's your guardian."

"Her what?" Quentin finally spoke up, confusion clouding his usual poker face.

"My what? You're making no sense," I snapped back, tired of being the one left in the dark. I shrugged off Dad's arm and looked at him. Waiting. Expecting him to jump in and deny the entire conversation. Deny Aunt Lucy's outrageous accusations and set the sloping room straight again.

Moving closer yet, she shook her head disparagingly. "You people are so pathetic."

Fed up with his sister's insults, my father bellowed, "Lucy, enough!" causing me to jump.

"How dare you speak to me like that? After everything I've done for you and your pathetic attempt at family life."

"After everything you've done for me?" He laughed the laugh of someone on the verge of cracking. "Every choice you've ever made in life has been self-serving. What I can't figure out is what your motive is this time."

This time? What is he talking about, *this time?* I hardly recognized either one as they went at each other like long time rivals.

She walked up to his face and quietly hissed, "You are so lost in the dark Peter, without my help, it will take a small miracle for you and your family to claw your way out."

I wanted to step in, protect my dad from her harsh words, but I was a yo-yo being pulled up and down at the whim of others.

I was done.

"Stop it! Both of you!" I yelled, unable to listen to their petulant words any longer. I backed up. Away from them. Away from the noise I couldn't control. "Are you saying you both knew about this? You both knew that it could happen to me? And that the only reason Quentin has appeared is because he is somehow tied to what I'm seeing?"

"Cee." Dad's voice softened, his eyes searching for me. "It's not that simple. It's going to take time to explain . . ."

"Explain?" my voice rose near hysteria. "Don't you think I deserved an explanation before I went sliding off the deep end? Before I managed to disrupt and ruin Quentin's life."

"Yes, you did," my aunt gloated, crossing her arms over her chest. In that moment I wanted to slap her and tear the smug look from her eyes. "But your father has never been forthcoming when it comes to our family. It's easier to pretend we don't exist, than to be labeled a fool."

"Enough, Lucy! You have no idea what you are talking about."

"I know exactly what I'm talking about," she snapped back. "We've never been good enough for you, Peter."

I was done, unable to take any more for their arguing, their lies, their words labeling me as an outcast. And like a mere twenty-four hours before, I turned and stormed from the house, but not before I heard Quentin say, "Let her go. Her legs won't get her very far."

CHAPTER
20

The unrelenting wind whipped around me, swirling damp leaves up before striking them lifeless to the ground. The frenzied movement mirrored everything inside me. I stood paralyzed in the middle of the driveway, the pain in my legs leaving them useless, the pain of their lies incapacitating.

Sheer will finally trudged my feet forward — one foot in front of the other — up the stairs to the only sanctuary I knew. I threw open the door, not bothering to close it behind me.

My eyes darted around the dim room in dismay, begging for something familiar to jump out, something that felt like me, but it had changed. The walls were foreign. The art belonged to someone who knew who she was,

someone who was sure of herself, who, without a doubt, knew what her gifts were.

Did my mom know? Had she held tight to Dad's secrets, keeping me in the dark? The single thought stole my last ounce of courage, nearly causing the ground to rise and swallow me. I'd always been so certain of our bond — my running women, their disjointed energy. Now the sand was crumbling, her strength slipping from my grasp.

A blank canvas stared at me from the middle of the art table. The stretch of white was blinding. It taunted the darkness inside of me as it tipped the words in my head, riddling them into nonsensical streams.

Fearful the canvas would be my undoing, I reached a shaky hand into a drawer and pulled out a tube of raw umber. The cap bit at my trembling fingers as I tried to twist it off. Unable to make my fingers work, I clamped my teeth down around the lid and wrenched it off, squeezing a large mound of brown onto the center of the canvas. I stared at it but couldn't see. I couldn't understand how I had lived for seventeen years and not had an inkling of what lurked inside me.

My finger poked at the rise of paint, bursting a hole through the center, collapsing the sides. The acrylic clung to my skin, coating me with its murkiness. She should be here. Protecting me. She shouldn't have left me here alone with them. Alone with myself.

Alone.

I squeezed out more paint. I pushed and pulled, using all of my fingers, giving the color life and taking it away. Autumn flashed through my mind — her life in the balance, her fate resting heavily on what I saw. Agitated, I squeezed and smeared, squeezed and smeared, fanning the paint out in quick, jerky motions until there was no paint left in the tube.

My hesitation lingered only a second before I tossed the tube aside and reached in the drawer and pulled out another color — thalo yellow green, the cap unyielding in my slick hands. Again, I used my teeth, brown paint smudging across my cheek.

I emptied the full contents of the tube onto the canvas, its demise swift and painless under my frenzied movements. There was no direction. No cohesiveness.

The canvas — my mirror, my reflection.

The paint splattered, burnishing stains everywhere. My care had died along with each tortured color. Cadmium red. Bleeding. Puncturing rivets of pain. I pushed. I pulled. I tried to parse the words trapped inside me — visions, initial release.

Guardian.

Unable to cover the white fast enough, I leaned over and snatched the canvas off the art table, throwing it on the floor. I grabbed another tube of paint and knelt before the canvas, dousing it in mars black.

My rage and anger erupted, taking over my movements. I leaned. I scratched. Sharing my pain, releasing my frustration. I pounded my fists, leaving small tears in my wake. Every question, every revelation poured out brutally onto the canvas.

Eventually, the colors ran dry, exhaustion left in their wake. The mutilated canvas hovered on the ground, cowering in my presence. I collapsed to my side, my cheek catching the edge of my black masterpiece. And they came, one by one, sliding off my cheeks and forging a river across the painted canvas. A river of loss. Of deceit.

On they went, until I ran dry.

Tick. Tock. Tick.

Tock.

Time trickled through the room. The gray shadows bending into dark forms.

Waking me.

Entering me.

Chilling me.

I pushed my stiff legs out of the fetal position I'd been coiled in, and forced myself to sit up. My eyes slowly brought the disaster before me into focus. I stretched my fingers wide, the dried paint cracked, the sandpaper texture matching my coated insides. I stood and lifted the bleak canvas weighted heavy with emotions back onto the art table. It leered at me, pronouncing its victory over my undoing.

Out of the corner of my eye, I caught a movement. I spun around and faced the dark outline that sat perfectly still on the couch.

Quentin.

I was rooted, unable to move, the war of relief and burden raging inside of me. It was he who made the first move, lifting himself slowly, deliberately inching toward me.

There was a shift, a change in him, a gentleness I'd never seen in his eyes as he held mine.

"My dad was right. You're too quiet," I stated, trying not to be beaten down by the pity he exuded for the poor broken girl.

"An old habit." He reached out and fingered a clump of my hair coated in dry paint. "It looks like you need another shower."

"Yeah, a shower," I quietly repeated. The bath at his house felt like an eternity ago. I looked up at his softened features, unsure of what to say or do. I had no idea where the revelations of today left us, or what they meant, but I didn't want him tied to me because of a stupid family curse. "You don't have to stay, you should go."

I looked down at his black boots, waiting to see them move. But they didn't budge, not the slightest twitch. The clock continued to tick, the cold in the room causing my breath to create steamy circles around my face.

"Quentin, say something," I pleaded, unable to take the heavy silence any longer. "Yell. Scream. Kick. Fight.

Anything."

"Do you want me to leave?" he finally asked. "Is that what you want?"

"I don't know what I want. I feel like I've been dropped from a cliff and told to fly. Only, no one gave me any instructions before I was launched."

"I get it."

The laugh that escaped my throat was hollow. Empty. "How could you possibly understand? I've just been informed that everything I knew about myself is a lie and now, lurking inside me, is some strange phenomenon that has somehow forced you along for the ride."

"Hardly forced. And I understand better than you think." He took a step closer. "Why don't we go back in the house?"

"No. You don't have to do this. You don't have to be here." I slipped past him, past his care, past his gentle request, and moved toward the door. I didn't want his sympathy. I didn't want to trust in his words. I didn't want to care, only to have him fade away too. "You don't owe me anything."

"If you want me to go, I will."

I stood motionless.

My heart raced.

My knees close to buckling.

I wanted to set him free, to keep him from being dragged through the darkness with me. The words climbed up my throat and whispered out of my mouth

unbidden. "I want you to go."

The silence lingered. My voice screamed in my head for me to take it back and ask him to stay.

I didn't.

"Goodnight, CeeCee."

He walked out the door and I stood like a statue, unable to cry, unable to feel.

His steps faded into nothing until his engine was the loudest sound in my head, his tires spitting gravel as he tore from the driveway — tore away from me, my family, my curse — the sound slowly fading to silence. And still, I stood, unable to grasp how my world had just been shattered.

CHAPTER
21

I walked the painful route back to the house, each step a foot closer to the uncertainty that awaited me. My aunt's car was gone, as was Quentin's. He'd left just as I'd asked.

When I entered the house, Dad was sitting on the couch, his face filled with the same misery burning in me. I knew he heard me, but he didn't budge. We were both silent as I crossed through the room, stopping in front of Mom's painting. I saw it with fresh eyes. Torment and lies raging in the storm of blue. Love and hate where hard and soft wrapped around each other.

"Your grandmother used to paint her visions," Dad said, eerily commenting and breaking the stillness. I didn't turn. Instead, I wallowed in the nuances I'd never noticed. The texture. The strokes. "Her art allowed her to escape the hold the visions would have on her."

"Does she have them often?" I asked, unable to look at him and not be overwhelmed by betrayal.

"She used to. She used to see terrible pain and suffering. It would take over her mind, throwing her body out of control as she struggled to make sense of it." Succumbing to the despair I heard in his voice, I turned and watched him grapple with his words. His eyes focused on a face I couldn't see. "She would spend hours, even days, purging the images from her thoughts."

"'Used to'?"

Bitterness replaced the despair in his voice. "Your grandfather passed away five years ago, and along with him, the ability for her to see visions."

Confusion pulled heavily on my mind. "I don't understand."

"Cee, you have no idea how I wished this day would never have come." He exhaled loudly as his body dropped against the back on the couch in defeat. His past had caught up to the future. My anger kept me rooted in my spot, unable to console him. "I left. The day after I graduated from high school, and never returned. Not once. I will try to explain things as best I can, but there are holes. Things even I don't understand. I learned early on to close my ears and not ask questions. I didn't want to be a part of their world. I'd hoped to control in my life what seemed completely out of control in theirs."

"Sounds like a cowardly answer," I snapped, tired of people running and avoiding what can't be avoided.

"Probably, but like you, my mother didn't get to choose who her guardian was, leaving us all saddled with a mean S.O.B." A hard hatred coated his tone, spurring more questions inside me.

I dropped down on the arm of the oversized chair next to the couch, trying to hold back my exasperation. "You keep saying that word, 'guardian,' like I'm supposed to understand what it means."

"I can't believe we are having this conversation." He ran his hand through his hair, the movement mirroring Quentin's nervous habit. He took a deep breath and his words tumbled slowly from his mouth. "The visions are part of a system — a system that works in tandem with a guardian. You are seeing visions, because your guardian has been revealed. Your power of choice is limited by your guardian's ability to pull you out of the darkness."

"Darkness? Choice? What choice? I see what I see."

"Choice is life. It is all about your freedom to choose." The discomfort in his voice didn't make my freedom of choice sound all that great. "The choice lies solely in you. To choose which vision you want to see in its entirety. They will never fully form until you ask to see it."

"You mean literally? Like, "show me," and just like that, they will become clear?"

"Yes, literally."

I stood up, no longer able to take in the information sitting down. "This is not real. This can't be real. It's too off the wall crazy. Are you listening to yourself?"

"I know. But this is important for you to understand. You don't have to grant a single vision. You never have to see one. You can refuse them. Every single one."

"Will they stop happening if I refuse them?"

He shook his head with a sigh. "No. They never stop."

"And if I don't refuse them? If I ask to see them?"

"Your sight will be completely stripped away until your guardian restores it."

"Every time I choose to see a vision?" Although, after last night, I knew it was possible.

"Yes. Every time you ask to see a vision in its entirety, it is Quentin, and only Quentin that can release you by chanting, 'open your eyes and look at me' three times."

"How? Why Quentin? Of all the people in the world, why him?"

"I don't know the 'how,'" his voice faltered, leaving me less assured. "As your aunt mentioned, Quentin and your grandmother were both present for your initial release."

"Will you please speak in English?"

"The power of visions have been running through my family for generations. It is never known who in the next generation will carry the gift, until a visionary from a previous generation is present, along with the person who will become the new visionary's guardian."

"Aaahhhh," I yelled out, my hands anxiously shaking up and down, my feet stalking around the room. "This can't be happening. This can't be happening. This CAN'T be happening." The chant holding the crazies at bay.

"Cee, tell me what happened the night you met your grandmother."

"It was nothing. Grace and I were at the SAM. Quentin was there because he works there. He asked me if I had any questions about the art." I didn't expand on our real conversation. It was a lifetime ago, with another person. She didn't exist anymore.

"And?"

"And what? I felt a strange tingling crawl up my neck and the next thing I knew, I was face to face with Evelyn just before I passed out."

"Did you see anything before you passed out?"

"A bunch of color and than random images. They were fuzzy. Distorted. They made no sense."

"They weren't meant to be understood. They were the initial release of future visions waiting to be seen."

"Are you saying I have a back-log of visions piled up in my head?"

"It's not quite as simple as that, but yes, there are visions waiting to be seen."

"Why don't you have them? Or Aunt Lucy?"

He looked down as he scooted his body forward. Using the arm of the couch for balance, he stood and muttered, "Lucy has always wanted them."

And a light went on. "Is that what this was all about? Her sudden piss and stomp?"

"Yes," he said, walking along the back of the couch. "But that is of no concern to you. Lucy has always been

selfish when it comes to what she wants. She's my thorn to deal with, not yours."

My mind ached, unable to reconcile the aunt I saw today with the kind and generous one I've always known. I stared at him, his fingers tracing the lines along the back of the couch and in that moment, I realized he was a stranger, lost inside a body I no longer recognized. Leaving me completely alone, desperately wanting to outrun their crazy gene pool. "She can have them," I said tartly, before asking the question I'd been dreading. "Did Mom know?"

His head snapped up. "About the visions?" he asked. "No."

My shoulders dropped, my body sagging in relief. But my heart still ached. For her. For me. For Dad who had nobody. He'd hidden much, only to lose control of everything.

He stopped at the end of the couch, his eyes focused on the back deck. "Where's Quentin?"

"Gone."

"But not really gone, you do realize that, don't you?" The tone of his voice sent a wave of dread through me. "There is no changing the tie that binds you two together."

"Yes there is," stubbornness rooting strength in me. "According to you, I have the power to deny every vision, and so, will never have need for a guardian." Never have

need to bind myself to someone who does not want to be weighted down.

"If only it were that easy." I followed him as he made his way into the kitchen. He walked over to the table and did something I rarely saw him do. He grabbed a pen and a piece of paper and scrawled a few crooked lines across the page.

He turned and held it out to me, resigned.

I didn't move. "What is it?"

"Take it."

I grabbed the piece of paper and saw his mother's name and an address. "How do you know where she lives?"

"I may not talk to her, but one never forgets where home is." He dropped down in a kitchen chair, and in defeat said, "She can answer all your questions."

CHAPTER
22

I stood on the sidewalk and craned my neck up. The long flight of cement stairs felt daunting, even more than the old brick house playing peak-a-boo behind the thick hedge boarding the property. I re-read the address Dad had scrawled down. The afternoon salt air billowed up from the Sound, prickling my cheeks and pinching me to make a decision.

All week I had wished for someone to pinch me as I rolled through the days in an impenetrable bubble. Every morning numb and every night, exhausted from the stress of waiting.

Waiting.

Waiting.

Waiting for the onslaught. Waiting for the opportunity to deny the visions. Waiting while the normal facets of my life jumped in the backseat and turned fuzzy, driving far from reality. Because this was not reality, it was limbo. Worse than limbo, it was nowhere.

The same place Dad's sudden attentiveness had sprung up from. His constant checking on me grated down every raw nerve, serving as a constant reminder of his absence from my life up until last weekend. Even Grace's usual brash ways were unable to slip through my numbness. Quickly tiring of my funk, she flitted off, leaving a crater of quiet in my head.

I glanced up and down the sidewalk, half expecting Quentin to appear out of nowhere. His house couldn't be far from here, secretly tucked back on one of the winding roads on the south slope of Queen Anne hill. I couldn't remember where. But it didn't matter. He'd done just as I asked and hadn't turned back.

I looked up the stairs again and gave myself a countdown starting from ten. I took a deep breath at six, and before I chickened out, began my ascent as I muttered three.

A decorative iron gate waited for me at the top. Behind it rose a turn of the century colonial out of impeccable grounds, the panoramic view of the city and Puget Sound enhanced every brick and white shutter.

I pinched my lips together, holding in an astonished whistle. I couldn't picture it. Dad. Here. His formative years shaped by the formidable house. My insides were jumpy, my feet anxious to descend back down the stairs,

but too much limbo pushed me forward, across the half-moon driveway and up to the front door, using the brass lion knocker to announce my arrival.

Nothing. No movement or sound came from behind the door. As I was about to try the knocker again, the door creaked open, revealing the face of Felix.

Flashes of seeing his face at the football game gripped my chest in panic. I took an unconscious step back.

"Ah, CeeCee. An unexpected visit."

"I saw you . . ." My voice trailed off, now uncertain of what I'd seen. Or possibly imagined.

His eyes narrowed. "What was that?"

"Um, nothing. Is Evelyn home?" I sounded braver than I felt. I hadn't called. I didn't want any prepared speeches or risk being turned away.

"Please, come in." He pulled the door wide with a pleasant smile and gestured for me to step into a grand foyer that spanned two stories. I hesitated before stepping into the entry where a large chandelier drew my eyes up, and a heavy, mahogany staircase pulled them back down. Beyond the stairs, stood two dark columns that marked the entrance of a pristine living room glowing white.

"Why don't you wait in here," he said, motioning to the flawless room. "I will see if your grandmother is available." He turned on his heels and walked from the entryway.

"Thank you." The quiet crack of my voice bounced endlessly around me, confusing my ears and setting my mind spinning.

Move.

Heel. Toe. Heel. Toe.

Toe. Toe.

Each toe sunk into the plush white carpet, my jaw hanging somewhere near my chest. White was everywhere under the vaulted ceilings, except for the walls. They were a moving life form all their own. Every last inch was filled with a chaotic patchwork of art. Oils. Acrylics. Watercolors. A beautiful, overwhelming mass of creation. I walked the length of the walls, my eyes focusing on each individual piece, pushing the overwhelming numbers to the peripheral. It was the antithesis of Quentin's home.

"This is a pleasant surprise, CeeCee."

I spun around. Evelyn stood tall in the middle of the room. Her self-assuredness radiated through a paint-coated smock hanging loosely over a pair of crisp jeans. "Um, sorry to bother you without calling."

"Never be sorry, CeeCee. You are always welcome in my home." Without turning her eyes from me, she lifted a hand and said, "Felix, will you please bring us some refreshments?"

My eyes darted to the doorway where Felix lurked silently. "Yes, ma'am." I watched his back recede down the hall, sending a wave of creepiness down my spine.

"CeeCee, why don't you have a seat?"

The offer triggered my body like a command and I circled around a white wing chair, sitting carefully on the

edge. Gripping my knees, I nervously blurted out, "Did you know Quentin lives near here." Where did that come from?

"Yes, dear, I helped him find his little house on tenth."

Her movements were graceful as she lowered herself softly onto the white couch, unconcerned about what might transfer off her paint smock. Wisps of hair had escaped from a loose braid flowing down her back, reminding me of my own kinky hair madness. But while mine was infuriating, hers gave her a youthful look that mocked her grandma status.

"Although," she went on, "the fact that you know where he lives leads me to believe that something has changed since I last saw you."

"Not so much," I replied evasively. There was no Quentin before the night of Picasso, and there was no Quentin now. "How do you know Quentin?"

She scooted back on the couch and clasped her hands in her lap. "I've known his mother for years. She's a long time collector and art benefactor in San Francisco. I'm sure your mother knew her as well."

My world was shrinking. So many people I should have been able to reach out and touch, and now, a lifetime later, they'd all converged at once. Curious, I asked, "Did you know my mother?"

"I met her just once. On the day of their wedding." Felix silently returned and set a tray laden with iced-drinks and small pastries on the table. "Thank you Felix.

Will you please ring Mr. Weston and let him know I will be running late?"

"Yes, ma'am."

"You don't have to do that," I said, standing up. "I didn't realize you had plans. I can come back another time."

"Nonsense." She waved Felix out. "Mr. Weston will wait. You, on the other hand, may stay as long as you want."

I was flustered, heat painting a rosy glow on my cheeks. What were we talking about? Quentin. His mom. My mom. The wedding. I dropped back in the chair. "I never knew you were at my parents' wedding."

"I hadn't been invited. I came as Lucy's guest." Her reply was matter-of-fact. No hurt or sting resonating in the shun. She scooted forward, and clasped her long fingers around one of the iced drinks. Holding her hand out, she said, "Please. Help yourself."

I shook my head no, my stomach a swirling cauldron unable to take on food. "Are you saying you crashed their wedding?"

"Yes. I guess I did." Her smile didn't waver, but her voice was firm. "CeeCee, I have never been good at small talk or beating around the bush. I believe there is a reason for your visit other than the 'who knows who' game. Am I right?"

"Yes." It was a whisper.

"Do you want to tell me about it?"

"Um, well, I've been having, um . . ." Why couldn't I say it? All week long the word snagged in my throat, unable to clear my lips. "Seeing. I've been . . ."

"Visions, dear? Yes. I know that much already."

"What? How?" I asked in confusion.

"Lucy called to tell me it was you who finally saw where Autumn was located. But I was already aware of the initial release."

Irritated, I asked, "At the SAM?"

"Yes. It was obvious they had begun."

"Why didn't you say anything?" I stood, pacing back and forth in front of the windows, remembering that night. She'd offered me coffee. A business card and coffee. No hint, no inkling of anything else. "A heads up on what I should've expected would have been nice, rather than having to muddle through them and spend a painful finger pointing afternoon with Dad and Aunt Lucy."

"Would you have believed me?"

No, of course not. Who could spin a story as crazy as this and call it truth? But that wasn't the point. "Probably not."

"I knew you would seek me out, or rather hoped your father would be able to see past his anger to bring you for a visit."

It was my anger churning, my tongue threatening to step out of line. "But he can't see. Ever since the accident he's been blind to everything."

"It's hard to see through anger," she replied quietly.

"He didn't used to be angry." Life had been peaceful. Content. Before. My voice trailed off, "Not while Mom was alive, anyway."

"Your mother possessed a gift far greater than my own." There it was — a hint. The first twinge of sadness I'd heard in her voice. "Why don't you tell me about your conversation with your father and Lucy."

"It wasn't a conversation so much as pissing match," I popped off, regretting my choice of words. "Sorry."

"Ah, yes. Those two have a long history of sparring."

"I don't get it. Them. Their relationship."

"I suppose the competition your grandfather flamed between them did their relationship no favors."

"Dad doesn't think much of his dad. He never talks about him." Or you.

"Your grandfather had high expectations for both of his children. The burden of which fell squarely on your father's shoulders." She set her drink down and extended out her long legs, standing and moving near me by the window. Her look was wistful. Eyes replaying private memories I would never be privy too. "But Peter always had a delicate soul. He was never cut out for his father's business."

"What business?"

"Harold owned a finance company. One he expected Peter to eventually take over, but I'm afraid Peter's dispo-

sition was tipped too far in my direction when he'd been born."

I tried to picture Dad in a suit, conducting high power meetings, jetting from place to place. It was an image I couldn't paint. His nature was too forbearing, too down to earth, making he and Mom the perfect team. Inseparable. "Why didn't Lucy go to work for him?"

"It was a different time, dear. Harold's world was a man-powered world. He wasn't able to equate Lucy as part of it. Nothing could sway his firmly rooted sexist beliefs. And he was never one to be trifled with. Or opposed." Her lips screwed into a contrite smile as she swiped her finger over the ledge of the windowsill, wiping away the non-existing dust. "One child strived harder under his scrutiny, while the other was slowly lost to us. Only, in his eyes, it was the wrong child. Not the most idyllic of circumstances, I'm afraid."

We were quiet for a spell, before I offered, "I don't think Lucy's happy that the family genes skipped over her and woke up in me."

My grandma turned and looked at me, her face open and honest. "I suppose not. She wanted it all. Her father's world, and mine. She always craved to see what I could see."

"And my dad?"

She moved through the room slowly, coming to a stop in front of one of the art filled walls. She stood there, her

eyes grazing across the frames, piece after piece. "I think the reality of what I saw scared him."

"Because it made you different?"

She turned, her eyes glassy and pained. "No, because I almost died granting a vision in his presence."

Her fingers reached out and gently traced over the lines of a soft watercolor in a simple black frame. The piece was plain compared to its ornate neighbors. "We had been alone that day — the last time he ever agreed to go anywhere with me alone. I can still hear his voice, small and feeble, trying to pierce through my darkness while his little hand held tight to a gash on my head, blood pumping between his fingers."

My heart sunk. The ramifications of the scene she described burst forth. For her. For me. For Quentin. I swallowed, pushing away the image of a fearful boy kneeling next to his mom. Pushing away the image of Quentin watching over me, and the burden of responsibility he'd been granted without being asked if he wanted. "How did it happen?"

"He'd accompanied me on an art buying trip to San Francisco. A trip meant to be one night. Down and back. We'd flown out early and spent the entire day in and out of galleries. Never once did he complain or tire. His nine-year-old eyes were wide with wonderment. His interest piqued beyond the average viewer."

She took a deep breath, reliving the details behind her eyes. "We'd been on the outskirts of the art district, viewing a new artist who's work did nothing for me, but it sung out to Peter. The simple washes and muted pallet had him mesmerized.

"One piece in particular had caught his attention. He insisted we buy it. I'd stepped over to have a closer look when the first inklings of a vision waiting to be granted began."

"In your neck?" I interrupted. "Like thousands of sharp needles being shoved under your skin?"

"Yes, dear," she confirmed. "Always the back of the neck. Inevitably painful, as it was this day. When no amount of words would convince him to step away from the painting, I had to pull him physically out the door and down the sidewalk. The urgency of getting him back to the hotel safely pressed in as the first wave of images hit.

"I had to stop, catch my breath, and wait as the shadowy figure teetered in my mind before I could move us along. I was trying to outrun the waning afternoon light as we zig-zagged from alley to street the fastest way I knew how."

She stopped and moved away from the watercolor. "But there was no escaping. I was never sure if it was the stench of the alley, the fading light, or Peter's small hand in mine, but the vision hit again, catapulting words from me I had not meant to utter just then. 'Show me.'"

Her story fit like a glove. The words so familiar I wanted to throw my damp palms over my ears and run from the room to slow the hard thumping in my chest. I didn't want to hear more but knew I needed to know more. "What happened?"

"The vision knocked me over, my head striking something sharp on the way down. I could no longer see outside of myself, only what was being shown on the inside. Eventually, even that faded, leaving only darkness and Peter's fearful cries. His eyes witnessing a regrettable scene as the pool of blood under my head grew, pulling me into unconsciousness."

She moved back to the couch and reached for her drink, taking a long sip. The clink of the glass returning to the table fractured the tension in the room, along with the pain of her story. She shifted, brushed the creases out of her shirt, and regained her matter-of-fact demeanor. "Harold flew in late that night to release me from the vision, but the hospital, unable to make medical sense of my temporary blindness, insisted I remain under observation for two more days."

"Where was Dad?"

"He flew back home with Harold before the morning light broke."

"They didn't stay?"

"Harold was never one for bedside manners. He did what he needed to do and returned home with Peter."

"Why didn't you deny the vision? Then none of it would have happened."

Her eyes found mine and I knew she was affronted by the question. "I never denied a vision."

"Why not?"

Her patience for my questions was dwindling, exasperation present in her tone. "Denying a vision would deny me the opportunity of making a crucial, life changing difference in someone's life. One that could possibly alter the course of their future."

Her words added another layer of weight onto my shoulders. My thoughts shifted to the couple in the alley. I swallowed down my trepidation and quickly asked, "What if you're too late? What if you can't unravel the puzzle of the images fast enough?"

"Ahem." I spun around at the sound of the cough, to Felix, hovering in the doorway. His hovering tendency was beginning to bug me. "Excuse me."

I turned back to Evelyn. She granted him permission to enter with the smallest twitch of her fingers.

"CeeCee," she said as she waited for Felix to approach. "You can't expect to successfully understand each and every vision. But to not try is a coward's response."

Felix leaned down, quietly relaying a message that floated to me as garbled sounds.

"Yes. Yes. You're right. I will take it," she replied to his words while standing, smoothing the front of her smock. "I have a call I need to take, CeeCee."

Happy for the excuse to leave, I stood and glanced at my watch. "Oh, sure. I should get going."

"Felix? Will you please fetch me the Gilmore piece off the wall?" she requested as we walked toward to the entrance of the room.

He scurried over to the simple watercolor, carefully removing it from its perch, an obvious hole left in the patchwork.

She took the painting from Felix and held it out to me. "I want you to have this."

Instantly protesting, my hands came up, holding back the air between us. "I can't take that. It's too much." It may not have cost much in money, but it cost much in pain. It represented everything I wanted to deny.

"I want you to have it. Think of it as a birthday present." She pushed the framed artwork out to me again.

Dumbfounded, I reached for it and asked, "How did you know it was my birthday?"

"I may not have been a part of your life, but I knew the day you were born."

"Thank you," I said, walking to the door she held open for me. Curious, I turned and asked, "What did you see that day? The day you were with my dad."

"A woman teetering on the edge, ten stories up. She was contemplating suicide."

"Did you get to her in time?"

"We are not successful every time, dear."

I sat in my car, tears stuck somewhere behind my eyes,

unwilling to flow. My hands grasped tight around the steering wheel, a watercolor heavy with burden and responsibility lying on my passenger seat, taunting me. My plan of vision denial began to eat away at me. I leaned forward and banged my head against the wheel, trying to feel something, anything that didn't have to do with my family or what I might see next.

Fed up, I turned over the engine and wound my way west, cutting from one street to the next as I tried to find a road to lead me off the hill. My aimless driving landed me on tenth. Without conscious thought, my foot eased off the gas, while my head made tiny shifts left and right pretending not to look. But I couldn't help myself.

And there it was. His small white bungalow, tucked back tight between two large rebuilds. I rolled to a stop, a tightness forming in my chest. His car was nowhere in sight, the house completely still behind the windows. I was tempted to get out and ring the bell, but my rational side took over and I shifted back into first gear and drove away.

CHAPTER

23

Darkness had filled the sky by the time I pulled into our driveway. Grace's car was parked in my usual spot. I let out a long sigh. Grace. I'd forgotten about meeting up with Grace.

Gathering my wits about me, I grabbed the painting off the passenger seat and lifted myself out of the car. Grace's outline swaying on the porch swing came into focus as I neared.

"Where have you been? I've been calling and calling. You had me worried you'd driven off a cliff or something." My mind instantly pictured a woman teetering ten stories up. Grace leapt out of the porch swing, clutching a brown paper package. "This funk of yours has me envisioning all types of crazy thoughts regarding your mental stability."

"Hey, Grace. I must have forgotten to un-silence my phone this morning." I stepped up on the porch and she piled the rectangle shaped package she'd been holding on top of the watercolor. "You could have knocked and had Dad let you in."

"Tried, but he's not home. Tell me you didn't forget we were going out tonight." She looked at me with a look that said, *I'm going to be crushed if you give me the wrong answer.* "To celebrate you? Your eighteenth birthday? Re-member?"

I shook my head no and lied. "I didn't forget. I was just over in the city, um, looking at art, and lost track of time."

"Well, you're here now, thank goodness. You almost threw off the entire evening."

God forbid, I thought, and then squelched it, remind-ing myself that she was here for me. And to heap on a little more guilt, she brought me a gift. "What's this? You didn't need to get me anything."

"I didn't," she said, pointing to my barely legible name written across the packaging. "That's the scrawl of a serial killer. It was leaning against your door when I got here."

"Oh, thanks." Carefully balancing the watercolor against my chest, I turned the brown package back and forth in my hand, but there was no indication as to who or where it had come from.

Impatient, Grace snatched the package back and pushed me toward the door. "Come on. We've got to hustle up and get you changed."

"Are we in a hurry?"

"Yes! You have social responsibilities, Cee, ones you've been shirking lately. You left me no choice but to take desperate measures to remedy the situation." The word "responsibility" dropped on top of the ones Evelyn had piled on me earlier, causing my feet to slow under the weight.

"Scoot!" She pushed me through the door and up the stairs, muttering, "Why I bust my hump for you is beyond me. But someday, you'll thank me for saving you from a life of spinster solitude."

I should have been offended. Come back with an appropriate verbal lashing to counter her words, but instead, all that bubbled up were giggles, that morphed into hysterics, leaving me gasping for air. I'd just seen my future lined with walls of art, and spinster solitude wasn't far from it.

"Glad I amuse you so."

"Me too," I said between gulps of air, tears streaming down my face. "And thank you. For whatever tonight is. Thank you, friend." I threw my free arm around her, squeezing tighter than I needed to.

"About time I got a little love tossed my way." She hugged me back before taking the watercolor from me too. "Now, think 'warmth' when you're deciding what to wear."

I looked her up and down and knew she wasn't kidding. I moved to my closet and began rummaging for winter warmth.

"Where's the watercolor from?"

I glanced over my shoulder. She'd dropped on the bed, the package and watercolor sitting in front of her.

"Oh, um, just a local artist over at Pike Street Market." I tried to sound nonchalant as I continued to search through the closet for warmth. She still had no idea who Eveyln was, and I was not about to spin the tale out tonight.

"You should have told me you were going over, I would have gone with you."

"It was a last minute thing." Which wasn't a complete lie. I reached up and pulled out a sweater and coat.

"Do you want me to unveil the secret of the mystery package?"

"Sure," I said as I wandered back to the bed.

She made short work of the unwrapping process, and by the time I'd pulled my sweater over my head, my eyes locked down onto a black and white version of me, staring back through the trees. A tightness seized my chest, transporting me back to Quentin's basement. To the row of humanity. A row that ended with me.

"Cool pic. When was it taken?"

"Um, awhile back." He'd been here. Today. Unsolicited. Unrequested. Unasked. I looked out the window. He'd come completely of his own free will. A crack fractured through the cold, hard silence of the past seven days.

"You're just raking in the art." She flipped the frame over. There was a small note attached to the back. Her re-

cital voice overpowered the soft words of the message. "'I hope you find a peaceful place to be,'" she read. "Cryptic little note. Who's it from?"

Racing through the possibilities, I blurted out, "Foster."

Unimpressed, she dropped the frame on the bed and stood up. "I won't let on that I'm completely and utterly crushed that you've confided your 'whatever's going on' with your brother and not your best friend."

Which wasn't true. Foster knew nothing. I sighed. "I think the note was meant to be a joke."

"Whatever," she dismissed the photo with a wave of her hand. "You two are a strange lot. Is he coming home for Thanksgiving?"

"Yes."

"Great. Strangeness times by two." She grinned and headed for the door. "Toss on that jacket, birthday girl, we need to fly, fly away."

I phoned a message to Dad saying Grace was taking me out for my birthday and I would be home later.

"So, where are we going?" I asked as I dropped into the passenger seat of her car.

She smiled a Cheshire cat grin that would have made a stranger nervous. "That is for me to know and you, girlfriend, to find out shortly."

We pulled up to Sean's house. I didn't see any movement in the dark windows.

"I don't think he's home."

"He's home."

Within moments, he piled into the car and we made two more stops, picking up Avery and Dylan, whom I was now sandwiched between in the back. "Is anyone planning on telling me what we are up to?"

"Nope," Grace smiled in the rearview mirror. "You just enjoy being chauffeured around."

Our bulky layers were adding to the smoosh factor. The heat was climbing higher and higher under my sweater, making me hyperaware of Dylan's close proximity. "More like being squeezed between roasting marshmallows."

"Are you likening me to a soft, pudgy marshmallow?" Avery asked with a grin.

"Not you of course, just the circumstances."

"Then I must be the marshmallow," Dylan said, nudging his shoulder into mine. "I don't mind. Everybody likes roasted marshmallows."

I swear he somehow moved closer.

"Don't you worry your pretty little head," Grace replied. "We'll be in wide open territory shortly."

We wound our way down the familiar route to Point Robinson Lighthouse. I hadn't been back since before they'd found Autumn out in the boat.

As if reading my thoughts, Sean turned and asked, "So what's the story with your cousin being out here last weekend."

I had no idea. She'd avoided me all week at school and the one time we talked, she fiddled with her cast and

mumbled something about a dare. "I think she got talked into it."

"Those impressionable youth," Sean said sarcastically, turning back around to face forward.

"It was a dumbass thing to do," Dylan piped in, his forearm now resting optimistically in the valley where our legs were conjoined. "She could have drowned."

"Or worse yet," Sean added over his shoulder. "She could have been struck by lightening."

Uncomfortable with the conversation and the close proximity of bodies, the "what-ifs" were not sitting well in my psyche. I'd already played out every scenario I could think of, leaving me to wonder what might have happened had I not seen her. What if I'd denied the vision and no one had found her until it was too late? Evelyn's cold disproval of vision denial ebbed and flowed painfully between my thoughts.

"Are you cold?" Dylan asked as I inadvertently shivered.

"No!" It came out louder than I had intended.

Avery touched my arm. I wanted to jump out of my skin. "How did they think to search for her out in the boat?"

Before I could reply, Dylan leaned forward, casually resting his hand on my knee. "I heard the police got a tip from an anonymous caller."

I closed my eyes and took a deep breath. A sheen of sweat broke out across my forehead. The conversation felt

like an out of body experience, every word producing a wave of guilt. For what I knew and what I didn't. For what I shared and what I kept hidden under lock and key.

We finally arrived at the park. I gratefully tumbled out of the car, gulping in copious amounts of fresh air. The cold immediately sucked away the inflaming heat and left a layer of prickly chills.

We followed the familiar path through the woods, heading across the clearing opposite the lighthouse. As we crested the grounds, a large bonfire stood before us on the beach with about thirty kids huddled around.

"What's going on?" I asked, confused, my body still reeling from the drive over.

"A birthday celebration of course!" Grace volleyed back over her shoulder as she danced down to the fire and yelled, "Let the festivities begin!"

The crowd responded with a tribal cheer that floated up into the air. I was certain the party was more for her than me.

"Happy Birthday, CeeCee!" Grace's arms flew around me as I neared the roaring fire. Glowing faces watched me in anticipation, hopefully not waiting for a speech because I was currently at a loss.

"Do you like it, friend? Are you surprised?" she asked as someone handed me an orange concoction that smelled a bit like gasoline.

"Completely." Cups were thrust into the air, arms wrapped around bodies, and everyone started singing

Happy Birthday. I, at the moment, would have been happy for the ground to open up and suck me in.

With one last squeeze, Grace slipped over to Sean and scooted herself up under his arm. I took a sip from my cup, promptly fighting off a sputtering cough laced with fire. I had no idea what was in the cup, but it tasted horrible.

"Are you really surprised?" I turned to Avery's raised eyebrows peering at me, her arm gesturing to the group gathered around the fire.

"By Grace? No." I looked back at the fire, a new liquid warmth trickling down my arms. "The party? Yes."

"Well, even if you weren't, good job for not letting on because she's been planning this for weeks," Avery said with a knowing smile. We stepped over a piece of driftwood and sat. The heat of the flames painted our faces red. She leaned in and touched her shoulder to mine. "As she put it, she was, 'determined to bust your funk.'"

"My funk has been officially busted." I continued to sip the citrus, gasoline blend in my cup, the beverage pushing liquid heat down to my legs, softening the sharpness inside me. I contently watched the dancing flames. My eyes blurred them in and out of focus as they licked the night sky and disappeared in a veil of smoke, rendering the noise around us white.

"Is everything okay?" I could see Avery watching me out of the corner of my eye. "If you ever want to talk . . ."

I interrupted her. "Thanks for asking, but really, I'm fine." I was too relaxed to risk a step back into reality. "Just tired."

Dylan dropped down next to me, his side pressing up against mine. "What are you girls whispering about?"

"We're not whispering," Avery said with a funny little laugh. Simultaneously, Grace's laughter floated over the fire, bursting into our conversation.

I tipped my head back and forth and caught glimpses of her dancing coils, the ends tipped in red.

"But if you were whispering . . ." His gasoline laced breath wrinkled my nose.

"If we were whispering," I said, unable to stop staring at Grace's afro springing up and down with every shift of her body, "it would mean it was not meant for your ears."

He draped his arm over my shoulders and leaned in. His mouth pressed up against my ear. "I'm good at keeping secrets."

I heard his words, but I couldn't process them. I cocked my head and watched as the tiniest of sparks jumped from Grace's red-tipped coils. They shot up and dove softly through the air before fizzling out. It was mesmerizing, my own private light show, increasing in numbers, beautifully filling the darkness around Grace and Sean.

The idyllic show flipped on a dime, sending a rush of painful tingles up the back of my neck and a hail of flames down on Grace and Sean.

"Grace!" I screamed, pushing on the sand, on Dylan, on Avery, on anything as I tried to get my feet underneath me. The drink had floated rubber into my legs, causing my efforts to be stalled as her shadow was consumed by the rain of fire coming down. "The fire — watch out! Get back!"

Everyone froze, their eyes searching, trying to figure out what the crisis was. My body felt heavy and uncoordinated.

Piercing the tense silence, Grace asked, "What are you smoking over there, girlfriend?"

Avery grabbed hold of me and helped me to my feet. I refocused my eyes and realized I'd imagined the whole thing. "Sorry, um, I thought . . ."

Sean burst out in uncontrollable laughter. "Vanderbie, you need to slow up on that drink of yours." Everyone else joined in the laughter, my vision playing out like a bad joke. A bad nightmarish joke.

An exuberant shout came from the group. "Someone give the birthday girl a refill!"

Dylan wrapped his arm uncomfortably around my waist, genuine concern in his eyes.

They were the wrong eyes.

I pretended to join in the laughter, waiting until the focus was off me before slipping out of his grip and away to the bathroom.

CHAPTER
24

My feet tripped along the dark path, the waves of laughter fading behind me. I crossed the clearing quickly and moved behind the lighthouse. My eyes were dilated wide, adjusting to the shadows, my body amped to hyper vigilance mode.

A branch cracked.

My head jerked.

I stiffly paused. Teetering. Straining to hear.

But nothing came. No one. Only the faint hints of the bonfire group wafting through the air. I powered my feet forward, chiding my mushy imagination. The only person of concern out tonight was the one locked inside of my own head.

As I emerged from behind the lighthouse, the Seattle-scape twinkled back at me, slowing my hurried progress.

The contours of the city jetted brilliantly into the night sky, leaving the valleys simmering in murkiness. To the far north stood the Space Needle. Alone. Nothing but darkness billowed around its base.

Evelyn was over there somewhere. With Mr. Weston, whoever that was. And wherever they were, it felt far from where I stood. A different land, in a different time, that harbored figments of my memory while holding tight to the enigma that lived in a tiny white bungalow. I stepped closer to the dock, the thought of Quentin winging flutters against the insides of my body.

Had he known it was my birthday? I shook off the stupid notion. Of course he didn't know. It was a sympathy gift, placed precisely so he wouldn't have to see me — the crazy girl who sees her cousin adrift and random people being shot.

The breeze blew up off the water, giving my curiosity a nudge forward, the planks of the dock moaning under my weight. Was it still here? The boat. Waiting for its next passenger? Waiting for someone to boldly step in and cling to its tempting frame? Each step brought me nearer. The moaning louder. My heart danced faster with a new image. An image of me sitting quietly in Autumn's stead.

I neared the end of the dock, the crest of the moon sharing just enough light to make out the weaving pattern of rope around the mooring cleat. I stepped up to the edge, planted my feet firmly as I peered over. It was

there. Exactly the same. No hint of the joy ride it took the previous weekend.

I inched closer.

Leaned a bit more.

Bent further over the edge.

A hand clasped hard around my bicep, causing a surprised scream to escape from my lips as I wavered on one foot, my balance upset, the water looking to be my new destination.

"Are you crazy?" the male voice hissed, yanking me to him. A shock of adrenaline shot through my system.

Confused and off balance, I spit out, "Let go of me!"

I ripped my arm out of the tight grip and righted myself. I was face to face with Quentin. Inches apart.

My mouth, full of cotton, was unable to form words. *Where did he come from? How did he find me?* Frustration frothed to the surface and I gave him a shove back. "You scared the crap out of me! You CAN'T sneak up on people!"

He grabbed my arm, no apology extended. "You need to come with me," he said brusquely.

My eyes followed the lines of tendons rising off his neck to his beautiful face, deeply aware of the increased thumping in my chest. "Seriously, are you spying on me? What are you doing here?" I asked, trying to calm my voice.

"I don't think now is a great time for questions. The cops have arrived."

Over my shoulder, I saw flashlights scanning the clearing on the other side of the lighthouse. Back and forth the beams of light went toward the bonfire.

"Come on." He tugged me away from the water and off the dock.

I tripped behind him, my legs forced to keep up. "I can't bail on my friends."

His halt was unanticipated. My forehead careened into his collarbone, shooting arrows of pain through my brow. Pushing on the pain with my fingertips, I looked up. Warmth from his breath bent gently around my face as his fingers gripped my shoulders. "You have two choices. Come with me or join your *boyfriend* and deal with your dad."

Boyfriend? What the hell was he talking about? My defenses slithered up out of nowhere. "I have no idea what you're implying with that snide tone."

"I don't imply. I ask. Are you seeing the guy who had his arm around you?" His unwavering eyes reached out and grabbed mine.

"Dylan? You think I'm with . . ." Laughter barreled out of me. "He's drunk."

"Are you drunk?"

"Not quite."

"You didn't answer my question."

"That's because there have been so many demands and questions in the span of two minutes."

He inched closer, his intimidating features catching my smart tongue, rendering it useless. "Are you or aren't

you with him?"

"No," I whispered. His scent swirled around me, tipping me sideways. "I'm not with anyone."

He didn't reply.

He looked beyond me and ran his hand through his hair. Finally, expelling a decided whoosh of breath, he grabbed my hand and maneuvered us into the woods. "Come with me."

We walked deep into the trees before he stopped unexpectedly and yanked me down behind a large shrub. My foot caught on a root, causing my rubbery legs to give out. I knocked us both over into a position of awkwardness. I scrambled to sit up and move away, but he righted himself first and snaked his arm around my waist, pulling my back tight against his chest. My face burned at the close proximity as his breath caressed the back of my neck. Inner havoc had taken over my insides.

Calm. Calm. Calm. This was not a big deal. Normal conversation. Just have a normal conversation. "Are you going to tell me what you're doing here?" Or not normal.

"Keeping you out of trouble." His arm went tighter around my waist.

My eyes caught sight of more beams criss-crossing over the clearing. "I wasn't in trouble until three minutes ago."

"It was a foregone conclusion. Teens, bonfire, and alcohol. It always equals police."

The havoc in my chest was slowly being pushed out by

annoyance. "You say 'teens' like you're so much older and wiser. Nineteen hardly qualifies you as the mature one. I can take care of myself."

"I'm sure you can," he said, ignoring my jab. "Have you had any more visions?"

Thrown off by the question, I paused for too long. The sight of the light show around Grace's head replayed in my head. "No."

"I don't believe you."

I tried to wiggle out of his grip. "You don't have to believe me. You don't have to be here. I don't need your help."

"You're right."

I pushed on his arm, grunting with the effort. "You can go back to your cozy little house in Queen Anne."

"You're right."

I could tell he exerted no effort what so ever to keep me in place, which fueled my steam even more. "You can continue your life just as it was before you met me."

"You're right."

"Are you going to say anything else besides 'you're right'?"

"No."

"Why not?"

"Because you wouldn't listen. You're too tight in the head to know when you need help." I swore I heard amusement in his voice, but I couldn't see his face.

"Tight in the head? What? What's that supposed to mean?" I struggled to face him, to turn, but his grasp held my back flush to him. "You're the one who always seems ready to bolt at any moment."

Lightening his grip minutely, he said, "I'd hardly call this bolting."

"Are you always this smug?"

"Only when others are too inane to ask for help."

I was done. Fed up. Without thinking, I threw an elbow into his gut, using surprise in my favor. With the back of my arm, I pushed him to the ground and whipped around, straddling over his stomach. "Enough, Quentin Stone," I snapped, pushing on his chest and waving my finger in his face. "I'm not a child. I don't need my hand held. I don't need a chaperone to keep me from scraping my knee or losing my mind. Which ever one comes first."

His lips curled into a half smile. "Hit a nerve, did I?"

"You definitely did not hit a nerve. I'm just telling you how it . . ."

My unfinished sentence hung as my upper hand was flipped, making short work of my moment of dominance. He rolled over me, assumed the position I'd just been in, and pinned my arms to the ground. "Would it be so awful to accept the smallest amount of help, Cee?"

Something in his voice shifted.

The edge was gone, leaving soft, velvety under tones that washed warmly over my face.

Unable to form any words, my body went slack and I nodded my head no.

"How about, just for tonight, you come with me." He paused and waited for my denial before adding, "And tomorrow? We'll figure out tomorrow."

The particles in the air had turned upside down. My breath was shallow as I stared deep into his eyes, unsure, not knowing if I could trust his words or his enchanting features that had softened with the offer. The offer of a tomorrow. I begged my tongue to say something. Anything. But the nearness of his lips made mine useless.

The distant voices began to grow, popping the bubble that had briefly consumed us. Quentin jumped to his feet, peered over the bush, and turned back to pull me up off the ground.

"We have to leave. Now." He pointed to the hefty hillside behind us. "Can you make it up to the top?"

"That way? You want us to go that way?" I wanted to go back to our former position. To have another chance to answer his question.

"We don't have much of a choice. The cops are coming down the path." He pulled his cell phone out of his pocket and taped the screen. A beam of light shot out the back, illuminating the ground around our feet.

"Any chance that phone is going to beam us up to the top?"

He gave me a courtesy smile and grabbed my hand.

We scrambled up the muddy slope, tripping on undergrowth and fallen logs. I was panting, hoping he wouldn't hear as I pushed myself to keep pace with his long strides, needing to prove, that if he could do this, so could I. By the time we crested the ridge, I was certain the pain searing through my lungs would cause my heart to burst from my chest.

I dropped my hands to my knees and sucked down much needed air. But there was no stopping, no resting. We remained hidden in the trees as he pushed us on, circling wide around the parking lot. The lights of the parked police cruisers flashed streams of red and blue through the branches.

We came to the edge of the woods. Quentin peered out of the trees and scanned the street. Again, I bent over, my labored breathing coming in gasps.

"You okay?" he puffed, stepping back near me.

"Fine. Just. Dirty," I huffed, brushing the dirt from my pants. "Why is it that I'm always in need of a shower whenever you're around?"

A rare smile appeared on his face. "I'm parked over there."

My eyes followed the path of his finger. I could barely make out his car camouflaged in the shadows against the forest backdrop. "Do you always park in dark corners rather than paved lots?"

"Come on."

We hurried across the street and climbed in, quickly aiming for Point Robinson Road. As we drove past the park entrance, I swiveled in my seat, and caught sight of a group stepping out of the woods.

Riddled with guilt for having ditched Grace and Avery, I pulled out my phone and sent Grace a text.

R U OK?
Saw the cops. Cut out the
back way. Caught a ride home.
Call me.

I slipped my phone back in my pocket, stealing a glance at Quentin. He was a rock, as usual, silent and unmoving, mocking the flurry of questions zinging through me. I clasped my hands and stared straight ahead. I waited. Patiently. My mouth clamped closed.

My bid at silence made it as far as my driveway but not before the car stopped moving. "How did you know where I was tonight?"

"Is that the question you've been churning on since we left the park?"

"One of them."

"I didn't," he replied as he rolled to a stop in front of the garage.

"Didn't what?"

"I didn't know where you were."

I turned in my seat to face him. "Are you sure? No special homing device? A connection that I wasn't made aware of?"

He chuckled under his breath as he put the car in park, the engine idling softly. "No homing device, just ears."

"Excuse me?"

"After I stopped by here, I decided to go down to the park. To the lighthouse."

"In the dark?"

He rolled his head toward me, his eyes filled with amusement. "Are you afraid of the dark, Cee?"

After my conversation with Evelyn, it felt like a loaded question. "I don't know anymore."

"You should find out." He shut the engine off before his eyes captured mine. "Although, a small dose of fear is a helpful tool for pushing forward."

He made the words sound like an invitation. "Why didn't you come over?" I whispered. "When you saw us at the bonfire?"

"You, um," he turned away, "looked preoccupied."

A picture of Dylan sitting close against me, his arm draped over my shoulder rose in my mind, and I blurted out again, "They're just friends. All of them. Just friends." Suddenly, it was important to me that he knew that. "And, thank you."

"For what?"

"For the picture you left at my front door." I turned my face back to his, a new peace flowing through me. "And for finding me."

"Happy Birthday."

"How did you know?" My body was tingling, and it wasn't because I was going to see any random visions.

"Evelyn."

No hocus-pocus, no secret guardian connection, just luck, coincidences, and my grandma.

We sat motionless, the tingles in my body charging the air. Unsure of what to say or do, I unhooked my seatbelt and pulled on the door handle.

As I turned to get out, Quentin's hand clasped around my forearm and pulled me back in. I looked up, the interior light enhancing every beautiful line of his face, stirring a cauldron of warmth inside me. He bent down and brushed the softest of kisses across my lips.

"Good night," he said quietly as he pulled back. "I'll call you."

My mind was reeling. "Um, okay," I choked out as casually as I could before stepping out of the car. I knew not to hold my breath waiting for the call as I floated to the front door.

CHAPTER
25

He was here, standing in my art room above the garage, staring at the chaotic painting I'd created the day I found out about my visions.

For minutes, hours, and days, the painting had sat heavy on my art table. Concealing the weight of my fears and the burden of never knowing what tomorrow would hold. Until, finally, I'd mustered up the courage to hang it on the wall and make peace with it.

"Why did you keep it?" Quentin asked.

Self-consciously, I stepped up next to him, soaking in the nuances for the millionth time. Through the rolling crests of black texture, tiny streaks of color could be seen escaping from the permeating darkness. It was nothing to look at, but I could see myself in it. I could see everything

— every hurt, every piece of anger, every drop of pain poured brutally onto the canvas. My reply was quiet. Honest. "It's the closet thing to truth I've ever painted."

His eyes found mine and held them. My heart became untamed before he moved closer to the painting, digesting more of my craziness. I blew out the breath I'd been holding and drew back to the art table, jumping to sit on top, freely drinking in the outline of his back. I labored to keep my façade of calm while my frazzled insides tried to understand why he'd agree to come here today.

He had called me the day after the bonfire fiasco, just as he said he would, suspending me in momentary disbelief.

And again.

And again.

By the fourth phone call, I worked up the courage to invite him to Thanksgiving dinner. Not that my family was such a treat, but it was family, and I knew he had none in town. It was to be quiet, small — me, Dad, and Foster. Foster was home, and that in and of itself felt like it grounded the unreal events of my life in reality.

He turned from the painting, his quiet words flowing over me. "It feels truthful."

Changing the subject, I said, "It's not too late, you know."

"Not to late for what?" His eyes smiled, sending a dart of heat to my chest.

"To back out of dinner tonight." I tried not to squirm under his gaze. "I had no idea my dad had made arrangements to go to Aunt Lucy's when I invited you."

I had envisioned a quiet evening over Chinese food, not painful family small talk at my aunt's. The last I knew, they weren't even speaking to each other. Now it was us, them, and handfuls of other island misfits.

"Are you trying to get rid of me?"

"No," I breathed out as he took a step closer. "I just can't make any guarantees about family fireworks."

His emerald eyes shimmered with amusement. He inched forward. "Fourth of July is my favorite holiday."

"I'll have to remember that." I inhaled a quiet breath through my nose.

The gap between us was diminishing. "How different could it be from what I've already witnessed?"

"No idea. I used to know. Or thought I did. Now, I'm finding I really don't know anything." I gripped the edge of the table, the blood slowly leaving the tips of my fingers.

His eyes gleamed. "You know you can see events in the future." He pressed his thighs against the front of my dangling legs.

Focus. Focus. His close presence making it difficult. "Well, um, I've got that going for me."

"And we know I can pull you back from the brink." His grin was wickedly lopsided as he slid his hands on either side of mine, our faces inches apart.

"I guess that's something," I whispered, my eyes vacillating from his eyes to his tempting mouth.

Back and forth. Back and forth.

I was spellbound. That was until Foster burst through the door, causing us both to jump. "Are you two hiding?"

"No!" I said too quickly, sliding off the table and stepping away from Quentin.

Foster's smile was mischievous, his sandy blond hair swishing low across his eyes. "Good, because I refuse take those twins on by myself."

"You know you love the attention." I used my best ogling voice before explaining to Quentin, "The twins have a strange affinity for Foster, well, Summer in particular. We're not completely sure if she understands cousins shouldn't get involved. I keep telling Foster he needs to explain . . ."

"Stop!" Foster interrupted, holding up a hand as the rest of his body shuddered. "I do not want any more of this conversation in my head."

"You started it."

"I only came up to tell you it was time to go."

"Why didn't you say so?"

"I just did."

As it turned out, it wasn't Foster we needed to worry about.

CHAPTER
26

We stood on Aunt Lucy's doorstep, painfully waiting while she and Dad greeted each other with a perfunctory hug. The voices of others floated out the door, blending us into a strange concoction of them and us. Even Foster noticed the weirdness and lifted an eyebrow to me.

I'd asked Dad the day before why he'd agreed to come, but the only answer I got was, "She's family." Which made absolutely no sense, because at the moment, the tension radiating off the two of them was drowning the rest of us. Not the most ideal of circumstances to bring Quentin too.

Nor was I prepared to deal with Summer's instant crush. She couldn't take her eyes off of Quentin as Uncle Russell made the introductions. I was certain she was go-

ing to pass out when Quentin reached out to shake her hand.

Summer leaned over and grabbed my arm, holding me back while the rest of the group moved forward to the main room. She quietly asked with starry eyes, "How do you know Quentin?"

I looked between her and Autumn who was standing idly behind us. Summer's crush was growing before me. "He's the guy I gave directions to at the park awhile back." Not wanting to destroy her moment, I added, "But Evelyn knows him."

Her eyes flew wide in surprise. "He knows Grandma? How is that possible? He seems way too cool to be hanging with Gram."

Summer had no idea of his existence or the fact that he was with me when I saw Autumn in the boat. But neither of them knew it was me who saw Autumn. That was information Aunt Lucy was holding tight to. Protecting them from my freakishness.

Unable to avoid the inevitable, I turned to Autumn and asked, "How's your arm?" It was a safe question.

"Okay," she answered. "The doctor said I get to take the cast off next week."

I wanted to know more. Why was she on the boat? What possessed her? Which friends talked her into it? But a deep discussion with her left Quentin alone with Foster and Dad for far too long. "Was it a bad break?"

"The doctor doesn't think so," she shrugged, offering no insight about the actions leading up to the injury.

Summer's newfound interest in Quentin could not be squelched. "So, does he live on the island?" She was hopeful, trying hard not to look at him as we walked into the room.

But I looked. "No, he lives in Seattle." Quentin's eyes found mine. As if knowing what we were talking about, he turned his eyes to Summer and deposited one of his smiles on her. A slice of envy shot through me, until I remembered he came with me.

I shook free of the twins and slid in between Foster and Quentin. Quietly I listened, my insides fluttering nervously. The atmosphere in the room was lopsided. I didn't recognize half the people. Dad was stoic, Foster interjected where he could, and Quentin remained quietly observant, his eyes constantly taking in the room of people.

My aunt circled the room taking drink orders, all smiles and pleasantries, no trace of the callousness she'd displayed at our house. Maybe I'd imagined it. Maybe Autumn's incident had sent her over the edge. She came to me last and asked with a smile, "CeeCee, would you mind helping me with the drinks?"

"Um, sure." My eyes flicked to Quentin before stepping from the group. I could feel him watching us as we walked into the kitchen.

My aunt pulled glasses from the cupboard and plunked them down hard onto the counter, causing me to flinch. Keeping her hands busy, she glanced at me with a hardness she'd kept under control until now. "So, CeeCee, have you had any more visions?"

Contempt dripped from her voice and chilled the room, putting me on guard. "Um, no."

She appeared buoyed by my answer. Mix. Pour. Stir. Her fingers never stopping. "Really? Not one? That's surprising." She spun and pulled a jar of cherries from the fridge. "It's been almost three weeks since, well, since we found Autumn."

"We?" I wanted to choke out, but instead played her game. "Yeah, about that." My fingers found a pile of cocktail napkins to fiddle with. We both knew exactly how long it had been since the Autumn incident, which left me wondering where this conversation was going.

"You do know that is quite unusual."

"What's unusual?"

"For that much time to pass without seeing at least a hint of one," she said snidely before citing her information source. "Mother never had long dry spells. Maybe the gift isn't as strong in you."

I refused to be flustered by her condescending B.S. I calmly called her on it, reminding her who had the gift and who didn't. "Evelyn said the length of time between visions varies in each visionary."

Her eyes snapped up in surprise. "When did you speak to Mother?"

Was she surprised that I spoke with her, or surprised that Evelyn didn't mention that I'd stopped by? "A couple of weeks ago."

"Did your father go too?" The faintest trace of alarm quivered through her voice.

"No. Just me."

Her shoulders relaxed, but the intensity of her stare worked hard to undo me. "I hope you are not taking this lightly. You have a responsibility. This is our family's most precious inheritance." Her eyes turned cold again. "No matter what the consequences are."

"Excuse me," Quentin's voice rang behind me. "Do you need any help?"

I spun in relief and could tell by the way he was looking at me, the question was intended for me rather than my aunt.

My aunt chimed in, her voice, like a switch, flipped back to cheery mode. "That is very nice of you to check-up on us girls and offer your services, Quentin. I see none of the other men had thought to do so."

I rolled my eyes at her loaded reply. Maybe her beef was with men.

She held out two drinks to Quentin. "These are for the twins," leaving him no choice but to deliver them. After he'd stepped from the room, she picked up two more drinks and trailed behind him. I was left empty handed.

Before she cleared the doorway, she shot a warning to me over her shoulder. "Just remember CeeCee, it is no longer about what is best for you. Selfishness, though it may run in your family, is not an option."

I was done. More than ready to go and end this shamble of a Thanksgiving, but we still had dinner to muddle through. What was Dad thinking?

Uncle Russell worked to liven the dinner table atmosphere with bad jokes. Each and every one fell flat on the tough audience. Across the bodies of strangers, Dad sat at the far end, his face unreadable as he quietly nodded at whatever my aunt was saying to him.

My leg pumped nervously. Up, down. Up, down.

Light, like a feather, Quentin's fingers landed gently on my thigh. My outward pumping halted, but a new one starting up inside me. I glanced up at him and he gave my leg a gentle squeeze.

Barely able to think beyond the fingers lying on my leg, I heard Foster say, "Interesting, when does it start?"

"This weekend," Autumn replied, not really looking at anyone.

He looked across the table to me and said, "We should check it out."

"Check what out?" I asked in what I hope sounded like a normal voice.

"Winterfest. At the Seattle Center," he answered, his cell phone already in hand scanning for information. "Autumn said they have events running all weekend, in-

cluding a tree lighting." He looked up and nodded to Quentin, "You should join us."

I didn't dare look at Quentin. I held my breath. Waiting. Hoping. Not wanting to influence his response.

"Sure," he said. I quietly exhaled and caught the soft edge of a smile form on Quentin's lips. I noticed the hopeful eyes of Summer wishing for an invitation. None came. Foster was oblivious of the crush.

"Great," Foster said, continuing his search. "Looks like the tree lighting is at eight o'clock Saturday night. Ice skating, carousel rides, caroling — sounds like a chick paradise."

"Then why are you going?" I asked, thankful for his smartass banter.

"To get you off the island, of course."

"Of course. You are so kind to think of me."

"I know."

With Foster's attention back on his cell phone, the voices around the table dropped to quiet mutters. Aunt Lucy had given up trying to play hostess with a cheery disposition. I did my best to ignore the intense glances she shot me. Summer was the only one left trying to chop up the silence, and even her attempts crashed and burned.

Blissfully, the night did not draw out long after dinner. Dad was ready to go home. We went to retrieve our coats and Foster stepped up beside Quentin and me and

asked under his breath, "Is it me, or is something off? That was the oddest Thanksgiving dinner in history."

My stomach contracted around the food I'd loaded into it. I had no idea how I was going to explain things to him or where to even start. "Um, well, I'm not sure," I began nervously. Quentin's hand touched the small of my back in a reassuring gesture.

Foster cocked an eyebrow at my feeble answer. "You're kidding, right? You couldn't feel the tension between Dad and Aunt Lucy. I could have stabbed my fork in it."

My shoulders dropped in relief. His focus was on them. Not me. "Things have been off for awhile." I didn't elaborate. "I was surprised Dad had agreed to come."

"Off, is right." He shoved his arms in his coat and tossed our two to Quentin before walking to Dad with his.

Quentin held my coat out for me. "Thanks."

"Sure."

We stepped out into the cold air. I wrapped my arms tight around my chest, a circle of steam enhancing my apology. "Sorry. That was awful."

"I've been to worse."

"I haven't. It was never like that when Mom was around." Flustered by the thought, I quietly added, "I was never like this when Mom was around."

We drove back to our house in relative silence. Foster hashed out the details of Winterfest with Quentin,

who offered to have us over to his place for dinner before hand. In a surprising move, he extended an invitation to Dad.

"Thank you, Quentin, but I think you will all get along fine without me." My gut twisted on his reply. Was he saying he didn't want to be with us or that we didn't need him around?

Foster walked Dad into the house, leaving Quentin and I standing alone next to his car in the cold. I worked hard to control the flight of flutters winging around my chest.

Quentin looked down, studying me, and after a moment, asked, "What's your aunt's stake in your visions?"

"Stake? What stake?" I asked, confused by the question.

"There's something. No one's that maligning without a reason."

"There's no stake. She's just annoyed that the visions jumped over her and landed in me."

"I think it's more than that."

"Why?"

"Experience."

"You do realize you keep citing your past experiences as references." I tried to contain my shivering. "One day you're going to have to start sharing what qualifies them as authority."

"You better get inside before you freeze," he said, turning to unlock his car door.

"Are you brushing me off?"

He spun back around and wrapped his arms around me, planting a kiss on my lips. "Yes. I would prefer you not freeze to death before our next date."

A shy smile crept across my lips at the word, "Date."

CHAPTER
27

I ran. I painted. I folded and refolded every piece of clothing in my dresser in an attempt to distract myself, tamping down the encroaching jitters of a planned date. He had called it a date, but it wasn't a real date, it was a gathering, as Foster would be there.

But it was a first, if you don't count Thanksgiving. Because Thanksgiving was a shamble of what used to resemble my family. Up until now, my time with Quentin had been a series of coincidences and happenstances. But there were no coincidences, according to my aunt. "Everything in our family happens for a reason," she had said.

But her blanket statement was too easy. It didn't stretch far enough over pain and loss. My pain. My loss. My mom.

Restless, I climbed up to my sanctuary and buried myself in poetry. Books upon books, pages worn from another hand, my eyes flew over words I knew had been absorbed and read by Mom.

My fingers, poised to turn another page, froze. Over and over again, my eyes roamed left to right, reading and re-reading the heart of Rainer Maria Rilke:

Suddenly, from all the green around us;
Something — you don't know what —
has disappeared,
You feel it creeping closer to the window,
in total silence.

The words dove in and grasped at my fading memory. Her dimming face, her near silent voice, my unrecoverable loss, and the uncertainty of what lay ahead.

I ripped the page from the book and began a flurry of movement over a canvas.

Greens.

Golds.

Fingers. Brushes. I stretched and curled wire, the light outside my windows fading into night. Foster broke in, waking me from my manic tango.

"Jesus, Cee. You're a mess." Green and gold coated my hands. My fingertips throbbed where the wire ends had pricked them. "Is that how you're planning to go to Winterfest?"

"No," I said, feeling pacified by the release, the purge, and overwhelmed by the emotions. "I need to shower."

"Now would be a good time. We have to leave in thirty minutes." He stepped closer to the art table and inspected the eye of my storm. A faint whistle escaped his lips. "Cee, this is amazing. Mom would have loved it."

The words were enough to send my arms around him and release a sob I'd been holding onto, undoing the semblance of balance I'd tried to gain.

"It's going to be okay," he said, hugging me back.

"I don't think so," I heaved through the tears I left on his shirt.

He waited. And waited. When I was calm, he pulled back, forcing me to face him. His voice was quiet, yet authoritative. "Cee, Mom spent years holding up brilliant, fragile egos. Now is no different. Can't you feel her? In this room? In the paint? In you?"

"But I can't hear her. Her voice has faded. It's gone," I sniffed and dragged my shirt sleeve under my nose.

"Are you kidding?" He laughed his rejuvenating laugh I'd missed so much. It filled me — fortified me. "Every time you speak I hear her."

"Funny, Foster." I picked up my brushes, intending to walk them to the sink.

He touched my shoulder with his fingers to stop me, his face a mask of seriousness. "I'm not kidding. It wasn't until her voice was missing from the mix that I realized

yours is a near match. Same tone. Same inflections. Same cadence."

"It's not the same."

"But it's something." He stepped back and fingered my paint-coated hair, evoking a memory of a night, of a boy, of a black masterpiece. My body warmed at the thought of seeing him. "I think you'd better shower."

"Yeah."

CHAPTER
28

A sharp reminder of winter's early approach whisked through the air, threatening to drop flakes of snowy goodness on us. With my hands buried deep in the pockets of my down jacket, Foster and I dashed from the car to Quentin's front door. It was cracked open, a sliver of light cutting into the darkness, anticipating our arrival.

"He does know he's heating the outdoors, right?" Foster softly teased under this breath. He pushed the door wide, unleashing a loud, "Hello?" I trailed in behind him.

"Hey."

I heard him before I saw him. A quiver of delight bubbled in my nose, the scent of him everywhere in the room.

I stepped out from behind Foster and a second greeting bounced directly to me. "Hi, Cee."

My nervous fingers twisted and turned, picking at a ball of lint in the pocket of my coat, but my eyes were caught by his. "Hey. Thanks for having us over."

"Always."

Something had changed since the night of my black masterpiece, something subtle, in his eyes. The way he looked at me, it was soft and unwavering. Exhilarating.

Foster broke the trance between us. "Nice place. Did you just move in?"

We moved through the stark room, depositing our coats on the couch. My fingers trailed over the arm of the couch before touching my lips in memory of a night not long ago.

I glanced up at Quentin. He was watching me — my fingers, my lips — missing nothing. I could feel the heat flame up my cheeks as the corners of his mouth quirked up. "About a year ago," he replied without looking away from me.

"Really?" I knew Foster's linear mind was clicking down lists, trying to make Quentin's response equate. "I'm surprised Cee hasn't forced you to hang art on your walls."

Looking away from Quentin, an odd protective nature reared up in me. "Not everyone wants their place dripping with possessions."

Quentin shrugged. "I don't have anything worth hanging."

I was about to ask him about the art I saw downstairs when Foster asked, "Is this a rental?"

"No. Evelyn helped me find it." My heart ticked out of time and I forgot to take a breath. Did he just say Evelyn? To Foster? I cringed, waiting for Foster's brain to catch up with the name.

"Eveyln?" Foster asked.

She was so far removed from our daily context, it wouldn't occur to Foster that Quentin could be talking about *the* Evelyn.

Realizing what he said, Quentin eyes flashed to me.

There was no avoiding it now. "He means Dad's mom."

To Quentin, "You know Evelyn?"

To me, "He knows our grandmother?" Foster's astonished face raced to latch on to the words hanging in the air. His eyes flooded with confusion, searching mine for answers. "Did you know this?"

I forced a calm, steady, "yes" from my dry mouth.

With eyes wide, his face jutted forward toward me. "Have you met her?"

I nodded, my mouth dry as a bone.

"When?"

There was no escaping, so I answered truthfully. "The beginning of October. At the SAM. She came up to me and introduced herself." My words were filled with a flood of guilt. I'd never kept anything from Foster, especially since Mom died. Now there's much, too much he

didn't know. "I met Quentin the same night. He works there."

"Just like that? Out of the blue, she recognized you and introduced herself?"

"Something like that." But it was nothing like that. It was planned, executed, and delivered, because there were no coincidences in our family.

We three stood, staring, crossing unfamiliar ground. "Damn, Cee. I would think that would be information you would share with family members. Does Dad know?"

I didn't want to say yes. I didn't want him to be the odd man out. "Yes."

"You're serious?" he asked incredulously. "I leave town for two and a half months and my family turns into a bunch of secret hoarders. What other secrets do you have up your sleeve?"

My tongue tripped over my words before quietly saying, "None." I didn't dare look over to Quentin.

Graciously, he steered the conversation elsewhere. "I'm not much of a cook, but I've got a pile of take-out menus in the kitchen we can order from."

We followed him into the kitchen. My eyes danced over the counters and cupboards, landing on the now closed door on the other side. My senses flooded with images of my last visit, and my not so stealth descent into Quentin's darkroom. It felt like an eternity had past, rather than just three weeks.

Foster fingered the pile of menus. "You weren't kidding when you said you have a stack. Do you ever cook?"

"Rarely."

I dropped down at the kitchen table. Foster followed suit after they'd decided on Thai for dinner and sat across from me. "I can't believe you met her," he said quietly as Quentin ordered our food. There was no anger in his voice, for which I was grateful. "What's she like?"

My fingers knotted around each other on top of the table. "How do you mean?"

"I don't know. Is she evil, friendly, ugly, fat?"

"None of those, actually."

"Then tell me what she is."

I could see her, standing confidently in her living room and I started to spout, "Tall. Self-assured. Eccentric. Dazzling. Intimidating. Thoughtful. Arrogant."

His eyebrows shot up. "You got all of that from a single meet and greet at the SAM?"

"You'll have to meet her yourself," I said. "She makes quite an impression." Quentin sat down next to me, causing the now familiar erratic heat wave to flame up my side.

Foster's questions shifted to Quentin. "How do you know her?"

"My mom's an art collector. The art world is small."

"Grandma's into art?"

"Very much," I said, picturing the mass of creation hanging in her home. "Meeting her shed light on Dad's attraction to Mom and her world of art."

Foster blew out a low sigh and slumped back in his chair. "Art or no art, I think Mom and Dad would have still ended up together. Their connection was indefinable."

Silence trapped us in our reverie, until a knock startled us out. The food arrived, ending our conversation and diverting us to lighter topics.

After dinner, I excused myself to use the bathroom before we left for Winterfest. I walked down the hall, my words reverberating off the wall. *"Coward,"* I had called him. It felt like a lifetime ago. And yet, I still couldn't place my finger on what had changed — in him, in me — I was no longer sure.

I opened the bathroom door and ran my finger along the doorframe. The ripped wood was gone, as if nothing out of the ordinary had transpired. The room was exactly the same, minus the rumpled hand towel and toothbrush.

I relieved myself and made my way back down the hall. My pace slowed as I neared Quentin's bedroom door. A soft glow enticed me to peak and I gently pushed the door wider. The bed was made, the pillows in place, and the table and lamp exactly as they were. The dresser on the far wall was the same except for the addition of a small picture frame propped on top. With a quick glance over my shoulder, I slipped in for a closer look. I squinted at the black and white image as it came into focus and took form. Familiar form. The same familiar form as the

picture Quentin had given me for my birthday. I was startled to see myself staring back at me.

"Why . . ." The word whispered across my lips to no one. I couldn't make sense of it, because sense told me something that couldn't be. My eternal tug-of-war raged on until a feather touch to my shoulder spun me around.

Quentin. His face was soft, captivating. I had to tamp down the urge to run my fingers along his scar.

"Quentin, I, um . . . I was walking. The light . . ." I pointed to the light, but couldn't remember why. I looked back at the picture and then back to Quentin.

Gently, void of all pretence, he said, "I think it captures you well, don't you?"

"Um, yes." It was me, peacefully oblivious of the danger hanging directly over my head. I looked up at his face, etched softly under the hair that had fallen across his eye. I tentatively reached up, wove the strands through my fingers and pushed them back. His hand caught mine and held it to the side of his neck. A strong, steady pulse vibrated against my palm.

"Quentin," I choked out. "I don't know how . . ."

He released my hand to cup his own around the sides of my face. "Do we need to know the how and why of everything?"

"I don't know." Bursts were popping in my chest.

"Maybe it's enough for us to decide to trust in each other."

I didn't have an answer, or a thought. Everything flew out of my head. His scent distracting, his closeness alluring as his lips came closer. Closer. My eyes were glued to the curve of his mouth, soft and parted. My chest was close to exploding before his lips finally sealed over mine. I was reeling. Aware of nothing. Feeling everything. My body molded to his. Hard against supple, my fingers memorizing every contour of his back.

Through the pleasurable chaos, I heard a noise in the other room. I couldn't place it. It took a moment for my head to register that the noise was Foster. Quentin must have heard it too.

He pulled his head back and asked, "Are you ready to go?" I was certain the grin on his face mirrored my own.

CHAPTER
29

We braced for the cold as we stepped out of Quentin's car. Sandwiched between the guys, I snaked an arm through each of theirs, feeling content, like a bird about to take flight. The air bit at my cheeks, but the warm sound of carols floated out of the Seattle Center and found us on our brisk walk in.

Pockets of people milled around a sixty-foot tree that emerged from an imaginary hole in the ground. Through the branches, hints of a spinning carousel could be seen on the opposite side.

Quentin pulled his coat sleeve up and looked at his watch. "We're early. Do you want to walk around?"

"I vote for a carousel ride," I said with a grin stretched across my face. I looked between the two of them, both

of their eyebrows pushed high up on their foreheads. "What? Is it too much for you boys?"

"You're serious?" Foster asked as he tucked his arms tightly around his chest. "I told you this place was a chick magnet. Aren't we supposed to have young children in tow to be allowed on the carousel?"

"Oh, but we've got you, Foster," I said, and added in hopes of goading him into going, "Unless it's too scary for you."

"I'll go with you, Cee," Quentin said, his arm casually resting over my shoulders. "But the ride will cost you."

"Cost me what?" I felt certain I would agree to just about anything.

"Not sure yet. But I will collect." He was teasing. I think.

"You two are killing me," Foster said, caving to pressure. "I'll go. But only because the festive night seems to be calling for a festive attitude."

"Very generous of you, Foster."

We walked through waves of laughter to the ticket booth. Quentin consented to let me buy his one-dollar ticket since he wouldn't let us contribute to dinner. Queued and ready, we waited and watched as the line slowly slid forward.

Illuminations of light revolved against the night sky as jewels twinkled under a gold painted canopy. It held me spellbound. My eyes blurred the pirouetting horses in

and out of focus. Quentin inched closer, his hand sliding effortlessly into mine. Slowly, I leaned my shoulder into his chest, his voice resonating around me while he and Foster carried on a conversation over my head.

The tinkling organ music whooshed in my ears and morphed into, *"Que sera, sera, whatever will be, will be. The future's not ours to see . . ."* And she was there. On the white horse, dressed in her floral sundress. Her hands clasped tight to the pole. Her head thrown back in laughter. She was laughing. I could hear her. Joyous, delightful laughter ringing in my ears. She pulled herself straight and looked directly at me, bestowing a dazzling smile upon me. I felt her. Fully. I wanted to reach out, to touch her, but I didn't dare move. I didn't dare risk the illusion disappearing.

Inadvertently, I blinked.

Like a camera shutter opening in slow motion, my lids lifted and she was gone. Only the horse remained.

"CeeCee," Quentin said, pointing to the moving line. "It's our turn."

"Um, great." I straightened and followed the herd moving through the open gate. We sat three across, Quentin on the outside, Foster on the inside, and me centered between them on the white horse. We laughed. We went round and round, up and down. The delightful smiles of the children charmed us, allowing us to bask in the childlike wonder.

Slowly, slowly, slowly, the ride came to a standstill, depositing us at the exit. We stepped out the gate and headed back to the tree for the lighting ceremony. I heard the carousel start up again. I turned for one last look. Hoping for one last glimpse. She was gone, but not from inside me.

"What time is it?" I asked as we approached the tree.

Peering under his coat sleeve, Quentin said, "Seven-fifty-seven. Almost time."

We found a spot on a grassy knoll. Quentin stood behind me and I leaned back. His arms wrapped familiarly around my waist, holding me secure.

We spoke easily with one another. Waiting, anticipating the dark tower of branches to shine bright. The air stirred and something wet skimmed my nose. I looked up. In the distant lights, small, delicate flecks of white drifted down from the heavens.

I held out my hand to catch one. "Is that snow?" I felt a giggle bubble up from inside me.

Quentin and Foster looked up and started laughing.

"I think it is," Quentin said. "It's unusual for Seattle to have snow, let alone this early in the season."

"I really need to invest in a coat," Foster said, currently sporting Dad's winter parka. "I never did get used to wearing one when I was . . ."

I only half heard him as a tingling sensation started to creep up the back of my neck. I knew what it was. My

hands gripped tight to Quentin's arms, steeling myself, waiting. Simultaneously, the lights of the tree burst on, the cheers soared, and my mind was ravished by color and the swift shuffle of images.

I closed my eyes against the bright tree lights. My mind a blaze. A fire. A ring. Burning around me. I was trapped inside the licking flames. Only a shadow danced in and out of view. It reached out an arm before recoiling from my view.

My body tensed. I strained to discern each image hurtling by, but my mind was paralyzed, unable to force my voice to ask for more. The fire was moving. I was spinning. And the shadow danced in and out of reach. Taunting me.

The whirl of movement in my head caused me to lose my footing. My feet began to slide out from underneath me and I clawed Quentin's arm, trying to hold tight. His own grip around my waist turned into a vice. Through the noise in my head, I heard his muted voice calling, but I couldn't find him through the flames. The fire burned and burned. Burning until everything went black.

"Cee, open your eyes and look at me." Quentin's warm breath blew in my ear. "I'm here. Open your eyes and look at me."

A panicked voice pierced through Quentin's gentle pleas. "Is she okay? Should I call for help?"

"No." He was adamant. "Give her a minute." His bare hand stroked my cheek, pushing the shadows back.

Light seeped through the slits of my eyes, calming the storm inside me. My lids parted like butterflies, revealing beautiful pools of green on Quentin's face. Quietly we sat amongst the noise, cradled together on the grass. He held me tight, patiently waiting for the vision to pass.

"Are you hurt?" he whispered, his mouth pressed gently on the top of my head.

I shook my head no and buried my face into his chest, comforted by his musky scent.

"Do you want to talk about it?" he asked for my ears only.

Again, I shook my head.

"Cee?" Foster's voice broke through my fog. "What happened? Are you okay?"

I looked up and squinted. He stood between the tree and me, a halo of light bursting from his hair like an angel. I had to shield my eyes to see his face.

"I'm fine, Foster." I tried to push myself up. I needn't have bothered. Quentin and Foster were both swift to pull me up. "I just slipped on the wet grass."

"Why don't we get out of the cold?" It was less of a question and more of a command from Quentin. Not relinquishing his grip on my waist, he asked, "Are you up for walking back to the car?"

"Yes." The trip to the car was quiet. No one talked. Quentin didn't let go of me until he had the car door open and me nestled inside. The short drive felt infinite

235

as I tried to placate Foster's questions and ignore Quentin's concerned glances. We pulled into the driveway and I quickly stepped out of the car and bee-lined for the bathroom once Quentin had opened the front door.

Not bothering to take off my coat or turn on the light, I closed the bathroom door and sat on the cold toilet lid, chills quaking inside me as my mind staggered. *What had I seen?* My head dropped into my open palms. I tried to assimilate the fiery slideshow that teased me with its vagueness. Taunting me. Calling my courage into question for not having asked to see more.

I swallowed down the tears threatening to flow. I was the coward. I'd been so busy pointing my finger at everyone else I'd never bothered to look at myself.

A light knock on the door interrupted my self-berating. I knew it was Quentin. He didn't wait for an answer. Instead, he stepped in with a flood of light behind him. Our eyes fastened on one another before he closed the door down to a sliver.

He sat on the edge of the tub and reached out. Our fingers laced together as the vacuum of sound swallowed us and turned the void red. Fiery red. I desperately wanted a paintbrush. A canvas. A chance to purge.

So I did.

"Everything was on fire," I choked out. "I was trapped. I couldn't see. And there was a shadow . . ."

His grip tightened around my fingers. "What about the shadow?"

"I don't know, it just danced beyond me and seemed to watch me." Words spouted from my lips, but my eyes only saw fire. "Taunting. It was taunting me."

"Are you sure you were in the fire and not the shadow?"

"I'm not sure about anything." Except that I'm a coward. A chicken. Unable to help, even myself. "I felt trapped. But it makes no sense. The visions are not supposed to be about me."

"Do you know that for a fact?"

"Well, no."

"Have you seen anything else like this?"

"No. Wait. Yes." The bonfire. Grace. "At the park, around the bonfire. I saw fire raining down around Grace."

His grip loosened. "Maybe Grace is the shadow."

"Maybe." But the answer didn't fit the equation. I couldn't explain why. But one thing did fit. Danger. It loomed over me, waiting to pounce, putting everyone around me at risk. I let go of his hand. "I can't stay. You can't be around me. This vision, future visions, I don't know what it means, but I can't risk . . .if anything were to happen to you because of me . . ."

"Cee, what are you saying? You're not making sense."

There was an edge to his voice as he pushed his hand through his hair.

"My dad watched Evelyn almost die because of her visions. I can't ask that of anyone." My voice trailed off to a whisper. "Especially you."

"I'm not going anywhere." His voice was firm. He slid off the tub and pushed on my legs, kneeling before me. "I meant what I said. We have to trust in each other."

"But, the images . . ." I tried to protest.

"I don't care," he replied, his hands firm around my back, pulling me to him. "Together. We'll figure this out together."

"Why? Why would you purposely put yourself in danger?"

He didn't answer my question. Instead, his lips found mine and gave me an entirely different answer to my question.

CHAPTER
30

I sprawled out on the couch and stared at the ceiling, unsure of what to do with myself, my thoughts, my visions. I could hear the soft murmurs of Dad's voice as he spoke on the phone in the other room.

Foster had returned to school, but not before proclaiming that when he returned at Christmas, he expected to meet Evelyn. I'd wrapped my arms tight around him, not wanting him to go, but needing him to leave. I was drained. The pressure of holding tight to my secrets and not letting him in had worn me down.

"Try to stay upright, Cee." His eyes flashed with humor, with love, with a rejuvenation that restored the emptiness inside me.

Lost in my own thoughts, I hadn't noticed Dad's voice had gone quiet, until his ghost like presence startled me.

"CeeCee?" He stood next to the couch and talked over the top of me.

"Yeah?"

He looked down. His unseeing ambers looked directly at me. "What are you doing?"

"Laying here."

He piled his hands on the top of his cane. "And?"

"And what?"

"Are you doing anything else besides laying there?"

"No."

"Do you plan to remain that way long?"

"Is there a problem with me being here?"

"No. No problem. It's just not your usual style." He reached down, felt around, and gave my legs a push. He sat close, a hint of shaving cream tickling my nose. "Are you still going out tonight?"

"Um, yeah." Quentin and I were having dinner. "We're meeting up later."

"I think we need to create some ground rules."

I sat up, dread slowing my movements. "What do you mean 'ground rules'?"

"Cee, you already know my reservations about you spending time with him. Especially alone. I think he's too old."

"You also thought he was too quiet." The sarcasm was lost on him. "Dad, he's only a year and a half older."

"I understand that, but a year and half is a big difference when you've been living on your own. Speaking of

which, you are not to spend time at his place by yourself. Too much alone time is not good for teens."

A thousand shades of red morphed across my cheeks. "Seriously, Dad?"

"I'm not kidding. And no sneaking around to meet up with him without telling me first."

I swung my legs off the couch, my arms laced tight over my chest, mortified by the conversation. "Fine."

Neither of us moved as a mild appreciation for Dad's caring rubbed on my heart.

He broke the stillness first. "You never told me about your time at Winterfest."

That's because you didn't ask and I didn't want to talk about it, I thought. "It was fine. Crowded."

"Foster mentioned you slipped. Maybe even fainted."

"When did he say that?" I asked, flustered. He never told me he had said anything to Dad.

"Before he left. He mentioned it out of concern." Dad shifted, and leaned back against the couch. "Did you have a vision?"

"Did you say anything to Foster?" Panic twisted in my voice. I wanted to be the one to tell him, but I wasn't ready to divulge my new inheritance. "Please tell me you didn't say anything."

"No, Cee, but you didn't answer my question."

"Why now? Why do you care now?"

"I've always cared."

"Since when? Since Aunt Lucy confronted you and

forced my problems in your face?" I stood and paced. My arms itched. Anxiousness boiled out of my skin. "You've been nothing but distant since Mom died and now you want to know who I'm with, where I am, and what I might see?"

He exhaled quietly, controlling whatever emotions swirled beneath the surface. "You sound exactly like her."

"What?" My confusion from his reply sucked the steam out of my rant.

"Your voice . . . it, it sounds exactly like your mother's, even when you're frustrated." The crack in his voice splintered the wall between us. "I hear you and I find myself looking for Gretta. Searching for her . . . desperately . . ."

"But, we've always sounded alike."

"I know. Intellectually, I know, Cee. But when I lost one sense it heightened the others, driving home the almost perfect, beautiful match. Do you remember the day after the accident? When Lucy brought you and Foster to the hospital to visit me?"

I nodded, not sure where this was leading, but not wanting the painful memories to tear through me again.

"You came in and hugged me . . ."

The room turned raw. I bit my tongue. Hard. The bitter tang of blood rooted me in the pain of loss.

"You told me how much you loved me. And I didn't reply." He stopped, holding the air in suspense as he regrouped, chocking down his emotions. "I couldn't reply because the only thing my eyes would produce was your

mother's face. You said, 'hi' and I saw her looking across the table at me. You said, 'I love you,' and I saw her eyes, the way they crinkled when she smiled. You asked me how I was and all I could see was her hair, pulled up in that funny knot she used to do."

I gulped down my sob and whispered, "Why didn't you tell me this before?"

"Because I couldn't see past what I was hearing. My grief for her," he choked, "my love for her . . . locked me in the darkness my eyes created. It wasn't until Lucy was here, berating me for being such a louse of a Dad that a light of clarity finally broke through."

I didn't know how to respond. I wanted to be pissed, but I was tired. I wanted to forgive him, but time had changed too much, displacing me, forcing me on my own. He'd left me alone for so long, I didn't know how to be with him.

"Cee, will you please come sit by me?"

Baby steps of trepidation tripped me back to the couch. I sat, sucking shallow breathes through my nose. He reached out and wrapped his warm hands around mine. They were strong. Foreign, yet familiar.

"Cee, I'm sorry." A tear escaped and traveled a crooked path down my cheek, matching his own. "I don't expect everything to be as it was. It can never be the same. But I would like to try and build something new. To earn back your trust."

Trust floated like a lazy dove through the tension in the room. It glided to me and dipped, holding out an olive branch. But for how long before the wind carried it away on a new course?

"I don't expect an answer now. Or even tomorrow. But I want you to know, that you don't have to go at this alone. I'm willing to walk beside you. Everyday."

"This feels like a relatively normal evening," Quentin said from behind his menu. Even screened by the list of specials, I could hear the upturn of his lips teasing me, lulling me into a hammock of ease. "Although, you, who normally has twice as much to say as the average person, has said very little since I picked you up. Do you want to talk about it?"

He set his menu on the table and focused his crystals of green on me. "I'm just tired." Exhausted is more like it. My conversation with Dad had my feet straddled over two sides of a train track.

Unconvinced, his eyes didn't waver, except for slow, deliberate blinks that held me in his razor-sharp perception.

I picked up my menu to avoid his gaze. Item after item I read, but the titillating descriptions were no match for the quiet endurance Quentin had mastered.

"My dad decided to start playing Dad."

"How so?"

"By setting up visitation ground rules for you." I peaked over my menu.

Again with the smirk. "What are the rules?"

"Stay on the island, inform him of my every tiny move, and," crimson rose up my cheeks like a thermometer, "don't spend time alone with you at your house."

His eyebrow shot up before he smiled his dazzling, crooked smile. "You can't be surprised."

Heated, I replied, "Yes, I can. He's never cared. Not an ounce since my mom died, and now, out of the blue, he issues an apology saying he's going to be more attentive. Just like that." Quentin sat motionless, waiting for my tirade to end. "Please tell me your parents aren't nearly as lame."

Bitterness flicked across his eyes almost undetectable. It reminded me of how little I knew about him. "Are they?"

"Lame is not the word I would use to describe my parents."

"How would you describe them?"

"I wouldn't."

"Why?"

"Because some people cannot be summed up in one word."

"Do you ever see them? Spend time with them? Go home for Christmas?"

"No. They go to Barbados."

"For Christmas? Really? What about your brother and sister, do they go too?" I knew I was pushing a line he'd been careful never to cross.

He sat. Unmoved.

"I don't understand. You never see your family? You never go home and they never come up here?"

"Does it matter?"

His chiseled features, meant to deflect my questions, were fully intact. But I refused to be derailed. "It does to me."

An eternity of seconds slid by when he finally said, "They come north when my father has business."

"How often is that?"

"Not often."

I couldn't begin to imagine what his parents must be like, or what life was like for Quentin growing up. "Do they have any business trips scheduled?"

He lifted his menu and blocked his face before muttering, "Next week."

I reached across the table and snatched the menu out of his hands. "Next week? Your parents are coming to town next week?" My inflection was too high. My thighs pumping a new rhythm of questions through me.

He was slow to answer. "Yes."

"Will you see them?"

His fingers ran through his hair and stopped on the back of his neck. The hesitation in his eyes vibrated intensely between us. As he opened his mouth to speak, I leaned in, but the sound that came out morphed into Grace's voice.

"Well, well, well. It looks like our little bird grew a pair of wings and flew the coop." I spun around as my two worlds came crashing together.

"Grace, hey, what are you guys doing here?" They were all here — Grace, Avery, Dylan, Sean.

"Oh, no, girlfriend. You do not get to steal that question from me." Her eyes were trained on Quentin. I knew instantly that she remembered who he was. "What are you doing here with, um, sorry, in the chaos of that night, your name slipped my mind?"

"Quentin."

"Quentin. Of course. How could I forget the tender morsel's name?"

"Excuse me?" "Grace!" We both said simultaneously. I was mortified.

Undeterred, she slipped in close to my ear and pressed on in a mock whisper. "Correct me if I'm wrong, but he is the same guy you passed out on top of, right?"

"She what?" Dylan's words shot high, composing an entirely wrong picture in his head. "You," he pointed

to me and than shifted an accusing finger to Quentin, "passed out on him?"

"I didn't pass out on him," I explained lamely. "He just kept my head from . . ." There were too many eyes. All glued on me.

Avery was my saving grace. "It's nice to meet you Quentin. I'm Avery." She side-stepped Grace and held out her hand.

He took it. His expression Switzerland. "Nice to meet you."

She proceeded with a point and introduction session. "This is Sean. Dylan. And it seems you may have already met Grace."

He nodded to each of them.

Dylan asked, "How is it that you two know each other?" The possessive tone of Dylan's voice was not lost on me. I didn't dare look at Quentin.

Grace answered. "They are both lovers of Picasso."

Strangle. I must remember to strangle Grace. I rushed in with a softer version. "Quentin works at the SAM. Grace and I met him when we were at the Picasso show."

"Yes, but Grace was unaware that said person was ever heard from again."

Grace's corny third person response grated on my nerves. I wanted to roll my eyes, wave my magic wand, and make them all disappear. Instead, I chose to ignore her. "Are you guys staying for dinner?"

"Yes. Yes we are." She slid between the tables and pulled the one next to ours closer. She practically shifted her chair on top of Quentin.

"Um, I guess we're joining you," Sean stuttered, baffled by Grace's antics, but still choosing the seat next to her.

Avery bent down next to my ear. "Are you okay with this?"

My eyes searched out Quentin's. A perfect poker face greeted me and I said, "Sure."

I was certain the only person unfazed by the strange dinner gathering was Grace. On and on she went. It was an out of body experience, hearing her through Quentin's ears. Her words sounded like dribble, her all-important thoughts and opinions paled when compared to the experiences of the past two months. Were we all this childish?

I looked at each of them. My friends. I looked at Quentin, my . . . I don't know what. Our friendship was the most un-friendship-like thing I'd ever experienced. I knew nothing about him. His friends. His family. His life. He was an enigma, somehow beckoned by fate.

After dinner, I was quick to rush us out of the restaurant. Away from the noise of my friends.

"Sorry about that."

"What are you sorry about?"

I slid through the car door he held open and waited for him to come around to his side.

"My friends crashing dinner. It was completely unexpected."

He pulled out onto Vashon's non-busy highway to return me home. "I liked meeting your friends. It somehow rounded you out."

"But you barely said two words."

"I didn't say I was good at social interaction, but it was still interesting to see who you hang out with when you're not peering into the future."

Before I chickened out, I blurted, "I want to meet your parents."

His foot hit the break too fast as he pulled into my driveway. We both jolted hard against the seatbelts. "Not a good idea."

"You've met everyone in my life. My family. My odd friends. I've met no one who knows you."

"Evelyn knows me."

"That doesn't count because she's still part of my family." I spun in my seat and faced him. "I want to meet them."

"No."

His face was set, but approachable. I leaned in closer. "Please. I'd like to meet them."

He shook his head no, his eyes locked on my lips.

"I'm not going to quit asking."

"My answer will still be 'no' the next time you ask." His reply was laced in velvet tones.

I placed my hand on his thigh. "Then I'll just have to get creative with the question." A source of adrenaline kicked in. The air in the car charged.

A glint of amusement swam through his eyes. We were nose to nose, his breath doing warm laps around my face. The crinkle of a smile emerged.

"My answer is still no."

"I didn't ask a question."

"I was making a preemptive strike." He sealed the deal without any further help from me.

CHAPTER
32

"Are you going to take me with you to meet your parents?"

"No."

CHAPTER
33

"When, exactly, will you be seeing them?"

"The answer is still no."

"I didn't ask to come. I was just wondering what night I should not expect to hear from you."

"Thursday."

CHAPTER
34

"Is there any circumstance in which you would let me come along? A favor? A request? A look into the future?"

"No. No. And no."

CHAPTER
35

"What will you do when you see them? Do they come to your house? Do you go out?"

"We go out."

"Where?"

Silence.

CHAPTER
36

"I'm not going to crash your party. I'm just trying to get a visual on your evening."

"Canlis, we're meeting at Canlis."

CHAPTER
37

I lied. I couldn't stay home. Curiosity took an irrational hold of my senses and the plotting began. I told myself I would just take one quick look. Nothing more. I Googled Canlis. The restaurant was far beyond my normal stomping grounds. The pictures dripped with beauty and elegance. I dug through my closet, trying on every outfit I thought might be appropriate. I needed something that would allow me to disappear amongst the other patrons.

There was really only one choice. My year old vintage inspired sleeveless dress from a winter formal come and gone. The formfitting waist, scoop neck, and all over lined lace were dainty enough to pull off as upscale, but subtle enough for me to become part of the background. I grabbed the matching heels and slid them on, teetering uncomfortably. I kicked them back off and replaced

them with my tennis shoes. I'd worry about balancing on them once I got to the restaurant.

I stood in the middle of the room, my resolve faltering. What was I doing?

No. I could do this. I was just going to look.

One quick little look.

I stepped over to my dresser and opened the top drawer. My hand slid under my bras and underwear, searching, feeling. My fingers touched down on velvety softness and clasped around a black box. I pulled the hidden box from its resting place, and with care, pried it open, revealing a long strand of black pearls nestled on a bed of creamy satin. Beads of pain strung together, beads Mom always wore out, knotted at the end.

For strength, I slipped them over my head. They had been a gift from Dad to her on their wedding day. A gift Dad had re-gifted to me the day of her funeral.

I stood in front of the mirror, my imposter status staring back at me. Who was I kidding? I would never blend in. One look from anybody with an ounce of sense and I would be called out for who I was. A chicken. A teenage chicken, who had no business being at an upscale restaurant, spying on a family I knew nothing about.

"Quit looking," I muttered to myself. This wasn't a night of espionage. It was just one. Quick. Peak.

I covered the tell tale signs of my plan with my coat and headed down the stairs, grateful for once, that Dad could not see me.

I grabbed my keys off the rack and snatched up my messenger bag, slipping my heels inside. "Where are you off to?" he called out from the couch.

I spun around. My blood pumping. What am I doing? What am I doing? What am I doing? "Grace's. Just to Grace's. We've got a project due tomorrow we're working on."

I waited. My breath lodged behind closed lips. I crossed my fingers and prayed he'd accept the lie as truth and not ask too many questions. "Let's not make it a late night."

Air blew freely from my nose. "Sure, okay."

About to turn for the door, I hesitated. Dad's frame sat completely still on the couch. Doing nothing. Seeing nothing. Trapped inside his own spinning thoughts. He wasn't all that different from me. The dove floated by and I bravely stepped off the train track and walked over to where he sat on the couch. I bent over the back, my lips landing softly on the top of his head, my words a whisper. "Good night, Dad."

His voice was a croak. "Night, Cee."

I hustled out the door and sped to the ferry, boarding the six-twenty. It was a thirty-minute crossing and a twenty-minute drive to the restaurant if I didn't get lost. I was rolling the dice on when Quentin might be meeting his parents for dinner. Six-thirty. Seven. Seven-thirty. It was a bit of a crapshoot, but parameters I could work in. They would either be deep into dinner or deep into deciding on what to eat. Either way, everyone would be too distracted to notice me.

CHAPTER
38

Valet parking. I was completely unprepared for valet parking, and the attendant who was at my car door opening it before I'd decided if I was staying.

"Good evening, miss. You can just leave the keys in the car." And he waited, trained perfectly not to smirk at my old car as he held the door open.

So much for blending in. I was committed now. "Um, thanks."

Self-consciously, I pulled off my tennis shoes, tossed them into my messenger bag, and replaced them with the heels. I slung my bag over my shoulder and stepped out swaying. Every muscle in my legs worked to keep me upright and not turn my ankle on the first step.

The attendant reached his arm out to steady me. "You okay?" he asked.

Damn. "Yes. Fine."

My walk was slow and purposeful through the columns of stone, wishing to embody their rock strength. *What was I doing?* It had felt like a good idea moments ago.

I swung the door open and stepped into a different world, wood paneled in the warmth of nature and the fortunes of the clientele. Eveyln should be here. She probably has been here. She would walk in and own the place. I tried to channel the self-confidence she naturally oozed.

"Good evening, ma'am. May I help you?" the maitre'd asked.

"Um, yes."

He stepped from behind his podium and held his hand out to me. I stared at his outstretched arm. Why was he holding his hand out to me?

"Your coat. May I take your coat?"

"Oh, sure." I shrugged it off, my dress suddenly feeling old and out of place. I needed to recalculate my exit strategy, adding time in for a coat check. I quietly asked, "Could you please tell me where I would find the Stone party?"

He folded my coat over his arm. "Are they expecting you?"

"Yes," my voice croaked as I kept my fingers clasped tight around my bag so I wouldn't fidget. "Yes, they're expecting me."

"Right this way, please." He handed my coat to another attendant I hadn't noticed standing next to him and signaled me to follow him. We passed table after table. The view of Seattle and Lake Union sparkling through the wall of angled glass. I had not planned on an escort and had no idea how I was going to ditch him before he walked me straight into the hornet's nest.

I vigilantly scanned the room, trying to spot Quentin before he spotted me. But we didn't stop. We kept going through the restaurant to the far side where a staircase was tucked away. Violent waves of uneasiness surged through my stomach as we began to ascend the steps. Step after step, bile rose to a threatening level in my throat. At the top, we walked down a long corridor and stopped in front of a closed door.

This was not good. My heart was threatening to pound out of my chest. No part about this was good. I opened my mouth to tell the maitre'd that I'd made a mistake. I wasn't really supposed to be here. They weren't expecting me. But before any words could fall out of my mouth, a voice from down the hall turned both our heads.

A burly guy, with dark, slicked back hair and a pinstriped suit was striding down the hall, talking on his cell phone. "This is not going to happen. I did not okay . . ." His feet stopped, as did his mouth when he saw us. "I'll call you back."

"Good evening, Mr. Stone," the maitre'd said with a nod after he'd ended the call.

"Good evening."

Mr. Stone? My body was a mess. It couldn't be Quentin's Dad. He was too young. Maybe thirty. Maybe not even. I tried to shift behind the maitre'd undetected, but it backfired.

"I was just showing, Ms," the maitre'd turned around to me, "your name was?"

"CeeCee," I choked out.

"I was just showing Ms. CeeCee to the penthouse." We stood there. The silence hung heavily around us. Finally, the matire'd asked, "She is a guest of yours, correct?"

Burly guy's wolfish eyes roamed the curves of my exposed skin, the dress suddenly feeling like a slice of sheer fabric. "If she wasn't, she is now. I'll take her from here."

"Very well. Enjoy your evening, Mr. Stone."

"Thank you. I intend too." A shady smile filled his face as he held out his arm to me. "Do you have a last name, CeeCee?"

"Vanderbie." It was barely a whisper.

His brow shot up quizzically. "Vanderbie?"

I nodded. This was not good. Not good at all. My hand tentatively came to rest on his arm, shooting the temperature in the hall up an extra hundred degrees.

His face curled back into a wily smile and said, "Well, well, CeeCee Vanderbie. Welcome. I'm Tony."

He grabbed the handle and flung open the door to a private sanctuary hovering high above the dizzying view below. I was dizzy, struggling to focus on his outstretched hand, one that swooshed the air in fanfare. "And this is my family."

My eyes focused in on three bodies that rose from the L-shaped couches near the window. Two foreign to my eyes. The other familiar. Too familiar. Except for the savage expression that pulled harshly on his face. He too, was dressed in a dark suit, finely cut to enhance every taunt line of his body.

My mind reeled. I was trying to visualize where I'd turned left instead of right. A step backward instead of forward. I was paralyzed. Tremors began to quake through me as Quentin stalked across the room. Gauging from the anger that radiated off every hard line on his face, I was certain his plan was to tear me from limb to limb.

Tony was talking but I had no idea what he was saying. His words washed over me like white noise, whirling around with the rest of the chaos in my head. I completely missed the excuse of my arrival. On his arm of all places. " . . . she appeared out of nowhere, so I invited her in."

"Remove your hand from her," Quentin seethed at my side. I finally dared to look up and realized his eyes were not trained on me, but on the person holding tight to my arm. A grip that tightened with every ticking second.

"Ah, the mystery is revealed. You're a little friend of Quentin's." His condescending tone splashed down on us. He patted my hand lying on his arm but did not relinquish it, sending a flood of crimson to my cheeks. I was trapped. I wanted my arm back from Tony. I wanted Quentin to take my hand. I wanted someone to vaporize me. "Such surprising news for you, little brother. You have a friend. But not so surprising that you would make her walk into the den on her own."

His brother? This was Quentin's brother? I pulled hard on my hand, freeing it from Tony's grip, which only made Tony's smile widen further. I turned, intending to apologize to Quentin, but his eyes silenced me. A brutality I'd never seen poured out of them, setting alarm bells off through my entire body.

"She was not invited."

A painful truth for everyone to here.

"Enough!" The bellow came from across the room. A commanding presence also dressed in a dark pin-stripped suit took two steps forward. He was as tall as Quentin with blue eyes sunk deep beneath his thick, dark eyebrows. The lines on his face were chiseled and sculpted by a half-century of time. So much so, I didn't think a smile could alter them. "There is a guest in the room and I will not have you two airing your petty grievances."

Quentin's dad strode over to me and held his hand out, his towering stature intimidating. "Welcome, CeeCee. We don't often meet acquaintances of Quentin's. We

would be happy to have you join us." My gut wrenched as I shook his hand.

A soft voice from behind, balancing the testosterone in the room, called out. "Quentin, will you please introduce me to your friend." All eyes turned to her. She was beautiful. Her dark brown hair fell straight to her shoulders, perfectly framing her Mediterranean features. She was petite, fragile in appearance. Her body fitted perfectly in a gold and chocolate brown dress, the two colors merging at an embellished band.

Quentin grabbed my hand. It was neither caring, nor possessive, as he pulled me toward his mom.

"Mother, this is CeeCee Vanderbie." His eyes touched mine for the first time. His face a perfect blend of his parents—hard lines etched on a soft hue of olive skin. "CeeCee, this is my mother, Theresa." I couldn't read his eyes. I couldn't ascertain what was pulsing through him at this moment besides surprise and pissed-off-ness.

"Vanderbie? Any relation to Evelyn Vanderbie? Or Gretta?"

I hesitated, unsure if I should claim them as relatives. As my delay drew out, Quentin said, "Evelyn's her grandmother. Gretta was her mom."

A barely perceptible surprise glided over Quentin's mom's face. Her eyes darted for a split-second before they returned to me. "CeeCee, we are happy to have you here with us tonight. It has been too long since Quentin has invited a friend to meet the family."

I didn't know how to answer. I wasn't invited. "Thank you," I replied meekly.

"If you would please excuse us," Quentin said, pulling me toward the door.

Safety was beckoning me to stay in the room. I knew if I walked out the door, I risked a berating by Quentin I didn't care to hear. My head couldn't take it. Or my heart.

"Quentin," his brother called out with a snarky smile, "try not to scare her off."

"Tony, stop," Quentin's mother admonished with quiet authority.

And stop he did. But it wasn't by any of us. It was by the new person who entered the room, whose presence stopped all motion.

A man in his mid-fifties strode in. His charcoal suit and blue shirt made his steal eyes glisten in the defused light. I looked up to Quentin for understanding, but his eyes were vacillating between his brother and his dad, his savage lines falling back into place.

"Anthony. Tony," the man said, walking toward the couches with his arms out wide. "I had heard rumors you were both in town. How nice to see you."

"Bernard, what a surprise." Tony's voice was animated. He walked in front of Bernard, impeding his progress into the room. "We're just up for a short family dinner, otherwise we would have called you."

"Ah, the family," Bernard said, stepping around Tony. He moved in front of Quentin's mom and held his hand

out to her. "Theresa, it has been too long. You look love-ly." She lifted her hand to his and he brought it up to his lips for a kiss that seemed to linger. Quentin's dad took a step closer to her with a menacing look in place. The movement added to the already thick tension chocking the air.

"Bernard, as always, it is nice to see you." Her reply was quiet. Polite. Gently extracting her hand from his, she looked up at Quentin's dad and wrapped her hand around his arm, unshaken by the intrusion. Her demure features seemed to pacify the tension in his shoulders.

Bernard turned to Quentin and said, "I do not believe we have met. I am Bernard Kaplan."

Tony came around to Bernard's side and said, "Bernard, this is my little brother Quentin and his girlfriend, CeeCee. Which is why we're in town. Quentin lives here. We all came up for an early Christmas dinner."

Bernard held out his hand, but Quentin made no move to shake it.

Unfazed, Bernard turned to me with his stretched out hand. I didn't know what do to. Shake it. Not shake it. Politeness won out. I lifted my hand to his like Theresa had done. He, in turn, lifted it to his lips and brushed a soft kiss across the top of my knuckles. "CeeCee. The pleasure is all mine."

I pulled my hand away as faint tingles began to prickle at the base of my neck. I knew what it meant and I knew what I needed to do. And quickly.

Catching everyone off guard, I quietly said, "If you will please excuse me." I briskly stepped from the room before anyone could react, not daring to look back.

CHAPTER
39

I darted down the hall, searching for someplace to hide. A corner. A closet. A stall. But I had no idea where the bathrooms were. I tested two doorknobs in the upper hallway, but they were both locked. I was frantic. The tingling surged stronger up my neck. In desperation, I staggered down the stairs as quick as my heeled feet would allow. I knew the enviable was biding its time to barge in and take over.

I quickly passed through the restaurant, drawing the unwanted attention of those dining in the opulent surroundings, but my level of embarrassment was tampered by fear of being taken down in front of them by my visions. I had to press on, move beyond them, away from their probing eyes.

The front door was in my sights. I focused all of my energy on the handle.

As I crossed through the foyer, the maitre'd called out, "Miss, would you like your coat?"

I held up my hand and shook my head no. There was no time. I shoved the door open and catapulted myself into the frigid winter air. The cold wind bit painfully at my bare arms and legs. I couldn't believe this was happening.

The tingles moved harshly up and over the back of my head as I teetered on my heels, tripping across the parking lot, my messenger bag banging against my thigh. I had to find a place out of sight. A place to be consumed by what waited to be seen. I rounded the last of the cars in the parking lot, my body racked with severe quakes as the onslaught of red coated everything in my head.

The red morphed and bounced until it circled down into fire, trapping me in its perimeter. The menacing shadow danced just beyond the flames. I sunk to the ground, my knees pulled tight to my chest. Round and round it went. Burning. Fear rising in the smoke.

The blaze roared. Each image charred by the inferno soaring high into the sky. Trapped within the fire, I stretched out my hand and reached for the shadow. I tried desperately to touch it, but the deep walls of flames made it impossible.

Ask for it, I told myself, *ask to see the face.* I hesitated, fear crippling me. The words were embedded deep in my throat, snared in a trap of doubt.

Ask for it!

Just as the fire began to smolder, the sky opened up and rained down on the scene. Drops of water sizzled around the dancing flames, painfully striking my skin. Stab after stab. Stinging with each penetration.

Ask for it!

It faded, darker and darker, the shimmering rain diminishing the charcoal to nothing. And in a blink, it was gone. Burning with it my courage.

Unable to stop the flood of tears, my body rocked back and forth, shivering uncontrollably. I'd just been pounced on by the playground bully, and I had no one to blame but myself. I bit my lip to silence my escaping grief, to slow the wave of punishing pain. I had no business being here. I had no right to a gift that I wasn't able to embrace.

My hiccups slowed and I tried to wipe the watery mess off my face. I sucked in a deep breath and held it.

"You're on your own. This was not part . . ." I froze. The airwaves carried a muffled voice to my ears. An angry voice. I didn't think it was coming from my head, but I couldn't be sure. Then I heard it again. " . . . never. I will make . . ."

My ears perked up. My body on alert. My heart drumming in my chest.

273

An engine turned over as I reached up and grasped the lip of the car windshield in front of me to balance my unsteady legs. I glanced through the glass. Two glowing taillights floated through the night air and disappeared from sight.

I sunk back down and took a deep breath. And another.

Summoning what was left of my dignity, I forced my wobbly legs to stand and move one foot in front of the other. I counted each baby step in order to keep the panic at bay. I couldn't think about it. The thought of burning . . .

"CeeCee?"

I lifted my head, startled by the voice. It was Tony. Standing by the front door.

"What are you doing out here?" His voice was unnaturally even, cooling my already chilled nerves. His eyes wandered up and down my disheveled state.

"Um, I wasn't, um . . ." My eyes darted frantically, looking for anything to propel a story out of my mouth. "I wasn't feeling well. I though fresh air would help."

"In the cold?" His eyes moved beyond me, where they found something to focus on in the parking lot. "Are you alright, now?" he asked, leveling his suspicious gaze back at me. I did my best not to shiver, but my cold body and Tony's critical stare was making it difficult.

I was just about to answer him, when the door to the restaurant burst open and Quentin stepped out wearing

a dark, wool overcoat. My own coat dangled from his hand. He paused momentarily, looking from me to Tony, his face livid.

Without a word he strutted over and wrapped my coat over my shoulders and tossed his parking ticket to the valet attendant. "If you can have my car here in under a minute, I will triple your tip."

"Leaving so soon, Quentin? The fun was just beginning," Tony goaded.

Quentin didn't answer. Didn't snap on whatever bait his brother was luring him with.

He tried another tactic, one sure to provoke a response. "CeeCee, just because Quentin can't hold himself together, doesn't mean you have to miss out on a fine meal. He has no idea how to protect what's important. I would be happy to have you come back inside as my guest."

Quentin spun around, his fists balled tightly at his side. "Do you really think it is appropriate to be hitting on an under-age teen while your wife and son wait for you at home?"

Tony roared with laughter. "Quentin, you are still so naive. Surprising, really, after all of your bad boy antics. I'm not hitting on your little friend, although, if I was ten years younger . . ."

Quentin's fingers rippled, opening and closing the ball of his fist. "You. Are. Not."

Tony turned dead serious. His intimidating step forward signaled my body to slide backward. "Does she

know? How at the drop of a hat you're willing to betray those closest to you?" Quentin's shoulders rounded back, his feet moved into a power stance. "I'm just giving her the opportunity to experience what true loyalty really means."

I didn't know what to do. They were equal in stature, both poised to strike. With words. With hands. With past grievances. I was certain Quentin's fist would land in his brother's face. I panicked, edged around the front of Quentin, and quickly spit out, "He told me. Everything."

The unscripted line halted the action, pulling four eyes down on me. One set drained of its venom by my lie. The other pair I didn't dare look up at. I could feel the sting of their sharp focus piercing through me, ready to read me the riot act.

The standstill was broken further when Quentin's car pulled to the curb. An attendant ran to open the passenger door and turned to me expectantly.

"Quentin," I whispered, pointing to the lot. "My car is . . ."

"Get in." His severe tone left no room for argument.

CHAPTER

40

Quentin tore from the lot, yanking the wheel left. Right. Left. He zoomed under the Aurora Bridge and up the north slope of Queen Anne hill, his driving erratic, far from the quiet calm I normally experienced with him. I clung to the door handle, my mind revolving through a list of what I should say, what I should ask for, what I should tell him. I did a mental catalog of excuses, but they all came up thin. I couldn't look at him — his anger — as we flew past storefronts, blew through stop signs, and headed back down the south side toward his house.

His house. A wave of apprehension dove deep into my stomach and turned it inside-out. Alone. At his house. I needed a diversion. I said the only lame thing that came to mind. "I'm sorry, Quentin. I'm so sorry for making such a mess of things with your family."

A pin had been pulled, releasing a whoosh of air from Quentin's pursed lips. He looked in the rear view mirror and abruptly pulled the car to the side of the road. He sat. Motionless. His hands clamped tight on the wheel, staring out the front window.

When he finally faced me, I could see the resentment boiling in his eyes. "Did you think this was about you?" He pushed his hand through his hair as he worked to contain his composure. "This has nothing to do with you."

Anxiously, I replied, "What are you talking about? I showed up uninvited and ruined your family's entire evening."

"It is not possible to ruin time with my family. That was done years ago."

"I don't understand."

"You're not supposed to. You're not supposed to be here." The hard edge of his voice was laced with anguish.

Guilt coursed through me. "I know. I know. I'm sorry."

"No, you don't know. I purposely moved away from them and their convoluted world. I thought being alone and keeping to myself would be penance enough."

"Penance for what?" I wanted to reach out and clasp my hand around his, touch his cheek, but I didn't dare move. The fear of rejection rendered me immobile.

He didn't answer my question. His head dropped back on the headrest deflated. "I spent so much energy extracting myself from their world, I wasn't remotely prepared for you."

I was no longer sure who he was talking to. Me or himself.

"When we found out about your visions, I thought maybe, removed from my family, you and I . . . That your gift made us . . ." His voice faltered, the broken sentences dangled on his tongue. "It doesn't matter. My brother's right. You have no business being a part of my life. The only thing it will bring you is grief."

"That's not true." Fear popped in me like a firecracker, threatening to blast us from the precarious edge we sat on.

"You have no idea what you're saying. Or why you're saying it," he snapped bitterly. "You don't know me. You don't know what I'm capable of, or what I've become." I could taste the bitterness stuck in his mouth. Of loss and lies. But I knew something else lay under there, well protected from the harshness of his family.

"Then tell me. Tell me why you left San Francisco?"

He just sat, unmoving. Every breath we took, gagged the stillness in the car. I reached for the door handle, tempted to let the cold air slap us both.

"Cee," he finally said, looking at me, his face a ragged mess. "I left San Francisco because I knew if I didn't . . ." An internal struggle played out in the lines around his eyes, uncertain of what to say. "I allowed myself to be dragged down in my brother's crap, and it cost me everything. Everything normal."

I let go of the door handle. My mother's pearls rolled together under my coat, floating a sweet sound up to my

ears. In an instant, her graciousness, her strength, her compassion embodied me, signaling what was important. The strength I'd been looking for earlier came pouring out in abundance. "I'm not going anywhere. And nothing you can say is going to change my mind."

His laugh was menacing. Thunderous in my ears. "That's what's so messed up. Somewhere the gods of fate are laughing at us. At your long line of visionaries and guardians. Because someone summoned me to protect you from what's locked inside your head, but they forgot to do a security check on what's sitting next to you." I flinched unintentionally, his harsh enigmatic rhetoric catching me off guard. He turned to me, ragged beauty etched through every line, and quietly said, "Who's supposed to protect you from me?"

"You will." Confidence reverberated in my voice. I was done being left and there was no way I was leaving. Astonishing even myself, I crawled over the center console and straddled his lap—the seams of my dress straining under the pressure. I held tight to either side of his face, maintaining his intense stare with my own. "Because I trust you."

"I'm a thief."

"I don't care. I trust you."

"I've done time in the system."

"It doesn't matter."

"I've been shot. Should have died. Wished for a long time I would have."

I traced the line of his scar with the tip of my finger and quietly asked, "Do you wish that now?"

His eyes captured mine. There was no hesitation when he answered. "No, not right now."

"Good, because you didn't and here you are. With me. Away from them." I leaned in, my lips moments from his.

"But that's just it. It'll never go away. Not ever." He pushed me back as he attempted to regain control of the conversation. "I'm not proud of what I've done, or that it took me so long to extricate myself from my brother's bullshit. But every action has a consequence. And I will have to pay. Until someone buries me in the ground."

My thumb did a lazy circle around his lips before I pushed my fingers deep into his hair, my lips finding his. Sealing over his words. Accepting them as my own. He leaned into me, his arms snaked around my waist. Every kiss met by another. And another. The built-up tension of the evening poured back and forth between us. His lips forged a fire trail down my neck, spiking my blood like a drug. I leaned in further and quietly whispered in his ear, "You're going to have to trust in us to figure this out together."

His head came up, his smoldering eyes fastened to my own. "So it seems."

We held tight to each other, like two sides of a coin— he not wanting to look back and me, afraid to look into the future.

CHAPTER
41

A car drove past us, breaking the spell of our connection. I peeled myself off his chest and looked out the window for the first time since we'd abruptly pulled to the side of the road.

"Where are we?" There were houses everywhere, except for a small clearing directly across from us. On the far side was a small stone wall creating a barrier between us and the shimmering lights of Seattle below. The stretch of shining fabric rolled as far as the eye could see.

"Highland Park."

"Is it public? Can we look?"

"You want to walk around a park in the freezing cold?" He reached out and caught the back of one of my heels, his face pressing into the scoop of my dress. The warmth

of his cheek set my heart to racing. "You don't exactly have walking shoes on."

I pushed him back and reached over for my bag, whipping my tennis shoes up into the air. "Ah-ha! But I do have these." I slid off him and changed my shoes.

"And you brought tennis shoes because you thought you might want to go for a walk in the park?" His smirk was evident, even in the dim light.

"No. I brought tennis shoes because balancing on heels is not one of my gifts." Not waiting for a further reply, I opened my door and rolled out of the car. The chill was in full force, biting at my legs, but I ignored it as I bound across the street, pulling my coat tight around me. I ran past the industrial sculpture in the middle of the park to view the floating Space Needle that pierced the night sky. The structure, with its graceful, feminine bends, dared one to rise as strong and as bold. And tonight, it was ours and ours alone. No one else was here.

Quentin moved up behind me and wrapped his arms around me, his body buffering me from the elements.

"This is beautiful," I said, captured in the moment.

Unsure if he heard me, I twisted my neck to see his face. But his eyes weren't admiring the view. They were locked on me. He spun me around, pulled me tight, my body molding to his.

"I was thinking the same thing." His hand cupped my cheek, his thumb gently gliding over my eye. I leaned

into his touch, the gesture sending waves of warmth to the pit of my stomach. "You and that dress are not a safe combination. It took every ounce of control I had not to pummel my brother when you walked in on his arm."

His eyes burned into me, but not with anger. A shy smile crossed my lips. "I really am sorry. He found me in the hall. I didn't know how to leave without making a scene. It was never my intention to come between you two."

"Cee, you can't come between nothing."

I wanted to instantly understand, to know more, to shoulder some of his burden, but I knew I had to wait. He had to tell me in his own time.

"Quentin Stone?" We both spun around to the new voice standing behind us. A man dressed in a black raincoat asked again, "Are you Quentin Stone?"

Quentin held fast to my hand and took a step in front of me. "Why?"

The man lifted his hand, producing what looked like a badge. "We have a few questions for you."

Us? As in more then one? My eyes darted around. On the other side of the metal sculpture was another man, his head moving back and forth, scanning the small open space. Adrenalin lanced through me. Suddenly, the luxury of having the park to ourselves didn't feel like such a boon.

Abruptly, Quentin pulled me around tight to his side, slowly moving us away from the man. "Cee, go get in the car."

"What?" I spluttered, looking between Quentin and the man, my legs locked in place.

"Go! Now!" he barked, giving me a push, his eyes a determined fire.

I stumbled slowly, my head swiveling, trying to keep the two men and Quentin in sight.

"What do you want?" I heard Quentin ask as my paced picked up, racing with my heart, suddenly beckoning for the safety of the car. I ran around to the passenger side and slid into the leather seat, sealing out any noise.

I watched the heated silent film of angry gestures play out in front of me. Time felt infinite. The unknown pounded through my body like a jackhammer.

In the blink of an eye, chaos erupted as Quentin threw a punch, causing the man to stumble in pain. He took off at a sprint, heading in the direction of the car. Without thinking, I leaned over and pushed open his door. He slid in, revved the engine to life and tore off down the street, leaving the two men running out of the park after us.

CHAPTER
42

Quentin kept the accelerator pressed to the floor, whipping us around corners, expertly maneuvering through the narrow neighborhood streets, taking one back road after another.

"Quentin," I finally spoke having found my voice. "What just happened back there? Who were they? What did they want?"

"I don't know who they were," he answered evasively, his head a constant swivel.

I gripped the dashboard as he yanked the car hard to the left. "He had a badge. Don't you think they were with the police? What if something happened to someone in your family?"

"Then someone from my family would have called me." The answer made me feel stupid and naive. His eyes

were constantly scanning. The windows. The mirrors. Watching. For them. For someone who was watching us.

"Are we being followed? Did someone follow us to the park?" I couldn't stop the vomit of questions that poured out of my mouth.

"I don't know."

"Why did we run? I don't understand. Couldn't we have just . . ."

"Cee, I can't explain. I've got to get you out of here."

"What do you mean you can't explain?" My voice jumped an octave. "Are we or are we not being followed?"

His features darkened as he let out a string of frustrated curses. "I don't know."

"Then what happened back there?" My tone emphatic, unwilling to back down.

"It's complicated."

"Don't tell me it's complicated, that it's too confusing, that it's none of my business." Hysteria was threatening to unleash. "One minute all was calm and the next we're flying through," I scan the street, trying to get my bearings, "I don't know where. Where the hell are we?"

"Cee, just let me get you home." His knuckles were white on the wheel. His eyes everywhere at once as he muttered, "I just need to get you away from this fuckin' mess."

I clamped my jaw closed, sealing the rest of my questions behind my lips. I had no idea who I was sitting next to, or what mess he was in, or what he was capable of.

Our surroundings turned familiar. We eventually found our way under the viaduct, vaulting from one parking lot to the other along the waterfront, slowly moving toward the ferry. Quentin stopped five blocks shy of the terminal and jammed his car into a dark corner of the lot.

"We're going to walk on the ferry. I'll call ahead and see if I can get a taxi to meet us on the other side." He shut off the engine and stepped out his door.

"I can call Grace," I said across the seats.

"Bad idea. Never involve someone unless you have to. We don't want them to have another person to follow."

"Who is 'them'?" I yelled before he slammed his door closed. He hurried to my door and pulled it open. Flustered, I tripped out of the car. "You've got to tell me what's going on."

He didn't answer. He reached for my hand, but I sidestepped his touch. Unsure.

The denial stopped him cold. He grabbed my shoulders, his eyes boring into mine. "You know me. I'm not going to hurt you. You have to trust me. Remember?"

"You've said that to me before, but I don't think you know what it means. If you want me to trust you, then you have to trust me."

"CeeCee," he pleaded. "Please. Let me get you home safe, because if I don't . . ."

Something crashed down from the viaduct above us, locking my breath in my throat. We both jumped and

spied a rolling hubcap that came to a stop ten feet in front of us.

He grabbed my hand. I didn't pull back again. Shadow to shadow we traversed cautiously, the surreal evening morphing into a nightmare I couldn't possibly have dreamt up. Our pace was fast. Quentin's constant over the shoulder looking putting me on edge.

The eerie stillness under the viaduct felt off, leaving too much space in my head to imagine the worst. I was full steam ahead, when Quentin veered off course and pulled us up to First Street, away from the ferry.

"Where are we going?" I asked, regaining my footing as I tried to keep up with his pace.

"Through the people on First."

I assumed he would take the footbridge back across to the terminal, but we skated by it and moved swiftly through the bodies milling around Pioneer Square. They clustered in groups, laughing, completely oblivious of our plight.

We stopped briefly under the glass-covered pergola, but with a quick glance in both directions, he charged us through the red light and across the street. Clips of sound slipped into my ears, but none to alert me if someone knew where we were at this moment.

Abruptly changing course again, he glanced over his shoulder and pulled us up a side street. The horns of a blues band bled through the doors of a nightclub,

lamenting our troubles but offering no assistance. He looked over his shoulder again before we cleared the corner. Uneasiness rippled through my chest.

"Where are we going?" I sputtered through the breath I was trying to catch. I was too scared to look back. "Is someone following us?"

"We need to loop around." He pushed his hair back, the movement somehow unsettling. We came to the end of the block. Quentin let go of my hand and grabbed my upper arm, guiding me into another brick paved park.

Not fifteen feet into the park, a vagrant sprung out from behind a tree. My stomach vaulted into my throat from the surge of adrenaline as he sneered directly at me. "Got anything for me little missy?"

I recoiled.

Quentin was the poster boy of calm as he stepped in front of me and held up his hands. "We're just passing through."

"Too bad," the vagrant slurred, his stench burning my nose. "We could've had some fun." Rapidly bored with us, he returned to his tree.

"Maybe . . . we should . . . go back to the car." I was skittish. Out of breath. And not a hundred percent sure of who I was with.

I took a step forward, and another, but they were the wrong steps in the wrong direction, sending me careening into Quentin. I lost my balance, my right foot hung

up on his left. I was going down. Quentin's reflexes were quick, catching me in his grip before I hit the ground. He spun me to him and put me back on my feet. My arms flew around his neck for balance. Assurance. I wanted this to end, but I didn't know what this was.

As I steadied myself, I glanced over his shoulder. I saw him. The man in the raincoat. My body froze uncooperatively as I watched the vagrant mumble something to him for having crossed his path.

Intuitively, Quentin said, "Cee, we have to keep moving." He put his arm around my shoulders and quickly moved us to the other side of the park.

"Quentin, he's here. He's following us."

"I know." He made a quick glance back before propelling us forward across the street to an alley on the far side. My nose wrinkled. The rotting garbage strewn about the cobblestones assaulted every sense in my head.

"Quentin, why is he following us? What does he want?" I tried to keep up with him.

The old cobblestone alley was filled with deep puddles, forcing us to walk close to the buildings. Then they hit. Tingles at the base of my neck. I didn't know what to do, but knew what was coming. I heard Quentin mumble something about "everything Tony touches turning to . . ."

"Quentin." Dread rang in my voice. "My neck . . . I think . . ." Before I could say anything else, color flooded over my eyes and images ransacked my mind. Fire was all around me. The shadow reached in and out of the flames.

Rain pelted down, piercing my legs. They played over and over. I could hear Quentin urgently call my name, but I couldn't lift myself out of the horror I was seeing.

Fire.

The shadow.

The glassy rain.

"CeeCee!" I heard Quentin's persistent whisper in my ear. "Cee, you've got to find me . . . come on!" My body, which had been in motion, came to an abrupt halt, sending the motion of the images off-balanced. They pitched sideways and backward. Reversing order and spinning around again.

My nose fought a new musty smell as the images competed for my attention, my mind at a loss. But it was too late. They faded to black before I could ask to see more. My eyes fluttered open, barely able to make out Quentin's face. It was inches from my own as he carried me through the darkness.

Afraid he'd trip in the dark and drop me, my arms flew around his neck. He peered down at me and asked, "Can you walk?"

"Yes." Not completely sure if I could. He set me down, but his arm remained firmly around my side. "Where are we?"

"The Underground." He guided us down a narrow wooden path.

My eyes strained to see through the murky air. "Underground? You mean below the street? How did we get in here?"

"I picked the lock."

"Of course you did," sarcasm slipping from my lips.

The path was a complicated maze of hallways. Quentin moved with ease, never hesitating over direction. At the end of a long stretch, a defused glow of light highlighted the outlines of a door. Or rather a makeshift door. It looked to have been created with a sledgehammer through a brick wall, the jagged sides waiting to snag the arm of a negligent passerbyer. Focused on the protruding bricks, I didn't notice the eight inches of remaining wall along the floor. My foot snagged, sending me down face first. I threw my arms out to brace my fall, but not before my knee struck something sharp, zinging pain up my body. "Arrrhg!"

"Cee!" Quentin was quick to pull me back up. The sudden movement released a threatening wave of nauseousness. "Are you okay? Can you walk?"

"Um, I don't know." The pain was excruciating. I sucked in a sharp breath and forced myself to work through the ache. We hobbled along until we reached the glow of light. A grid of foggy, purple glass on the ceiling emitted the above streetlight into the underground.

Quentin sat me down on a pile of bricks gathered in a small alcove. He took off his coat and laid it over my legs. "Wait here. I'll be back for you."

"WHAT!" I tried to stand but the pain ruled my movements. "What do you mean *wait* here? You are not leaving me down here by myself!"

"I need to figure out what's going on." He pulled his tie loose, his voice all business.

"You can't leave me," I pleaded. I sounded pathetic, but I didn't care.

"I'm not leaving you. I'll be back." His hands clamped down on my face as he leaned over, planting a chaste kiss on my lips. Before I could protest further, he stood and I watched the outline of his form disappear into the darkness.

A shadow becoming part of the shadows.

CHAPTER
43

It was quiet, eerily quiet, raising the hair on the back of my neck as shadows stretched long and dark along the wooden path. I looked up. Above, people walked over the grid of glass, unaware that I was trapped below them with no clue of how I got here, or how I was going to get out. I had no phone, no nothing, as I had left my bag in Quentin's car. I lifted his coat and flexed my knee back and forth. Slowly, I slid my body forward until I found a sturdy place on the pile of bricks to plant my feet and test my knee.

I would not be left down here to rot.

I adjusted my weight, leaned forward, and pushed my hands on the brick. The roar of a bus rumbled down the street above, violently shaking the walls around me. I

dropped back down and held completely still, waiting to see if I would become a casualty twelve feet below.

My energy was being zapped by my overly strained nerves. I needed to move. I needed adrenaline on my side. I stood gingerly, holding onto the wall for support. *Where was he?* I took a couple of tentative steps as tears of pain escaped my eyes. *How could he just leave me down here?* Tears of frustration rolled down my cheek. *He left me.* Tears of loss landed on the floor at my feet.

I followed the line of shadows Quentin had vanished into. The light from the grid of glass began to fade behind me, leaving only darkness ahead of me. Instinctively, I reached out, my fingers walking over the rough lines of the wall, feeling my way through the dark. Bit by bit, my fear morphed and turned into outrage. *How dare he leave me! Alone! In the dark!* My heart was hammering a marathon, but I was determined to find my way out.

Something skittered across the floor in front of me. I froze and sucked down a ragged breath, thankful I couldn't see what it was. Or how big. My baby steps were agonizingly slow along the rough path as my hands continued their brail walk along the bricks until I felt a ninety-degree bend in the wall. I reached for the other side. A door. Which way?

I lifted my foot and kicked around to be sure there wasn't another ledge for me to trip on. My foot hung in the air, about to step, when an arm snaked around

my middle and pulled me backward, upsetting my balance. A blood-curdling scream fell from my lips before they were stifled by a second hand that clamped over my mouth.

I sunk my teeth down hard into the flesh. "Ow! CeeCee, it's just me."

I whipped around and pummeled Quentin's chest. "You left me!" Tears of frustration poured down my cheeks. Low "umphs" whooshed from Quentin's mouth as I continued my assault, his body flinching with each of my blows.

His fingers clamped tightly on my wrists and he said, "We need to go."

"What happened? Where did you go?" I demanded.

He didn't answer. Instead, he pulled me back in the direction I'd just come from.

Like a petulant child, I stopped under the grid of glass and crossed my arms over my chest. "I'm not budging from this spot until you tell me what's going on."

He spun around and walked back to me. "We need to get you cleaned up and back home. That is the only thing that matters right now. I have to get you home safe." It was then I noticed a diagonal cut through a puffy, dark shadow under his eye. I touched the misshapen patch of skin with the tips of my fingers. He winced.

Lowering my hand, I said even more adamantly, "I'm not budging."

He stared at me long and hard with a look meant to scare me. But I was more afraid of what was above ground than I was of Quentin's anger. "I went back up to First Avenue and circled around, looking for the guy following us."

"You went looking for him?" I interrupted, my eyes wide in disbelief. "No one goes looking for . . ."

He held his hand up to silence me. "I found him. Tried to pin him to the wall to find out what he wanted, but the other guy he was with came at me from behind."

I don't know why I did it, but I reached for his hands and held them up, his coat slipping to the floor. Both sets of knuckles were scraped and bloodied. "Your hands . . ." He quickly pulled them from my view.

"They're fine."

"Who were they?" my voice demanded. "What did they want?"

"I don't know. I don't know who they were. I don't know what they wanted."

"You have to have some idea." My irritation was mounting by the lack of information.

He stared at me, his face set like stone, except for the muscles that rippled his scar in and out of place. After a heavy sigh, he said, "I never should have approached you that night of the SAM. I should have kept to myself and walked out of the room. But you just stood there, staring at those running women, your pain as obvious as

the colors in the painting." His voice faded off as he bent down and grabbed his coat. Angrily, he shoved his arms into the armholes. "You shouldn't be here. You shouldn't be involved in this. You should be home . . . painting. Or hanging out with your friends. I have no idea who those men were. My best guess is that it has to do with my brother and the man who barged in on dinner."

"Why would they follow you?"

"To get to my brother."

We stood perfectly still, staring at each other. Somewhere in the distance, the faint cawing of seagulls took me back to the lighthouse. To the picture of peace Quentin snapped of me. "It wouldn't have mattered," I finally said.

"What wouldn't have mattered?"

"It wouldn't have mattered if you'd walked away the night of the Picasso show." I took a step closer to him.

"Why not?"

"Because if it wasn't the SAM, it would have been another place. And if it wasn't there, then it would have been someplace else," I said, my body inches from his. "Eventually, you wouldn't have been able to walk away." I rested my head against him, my arms looping around his chest.

A hiss of air escaped his lips. "Cee, you have to let me go."

My arms dropped limply to my side. I couldn't look at him. My heart ached as I registered his words. Words

that lanced deep in the pit of my stomach and turned it cold.

"Cee, I meant you literally needed to let go of me. I think I broke a rib." He cupped my face, his thumbs pressing lightly on my cheekbones. "I said I 'should have' walked away, not that I could have."

It was a soft kiss he brushed across my lips. Enough to get me home. "Let's get you cleaned up and home before anything else can happen."

"Won't they be waiting?"

"Maybe, but they won't find us."

How does he know this? Why is he always so confident? "You will explain, right? Someday. Soon. Right?"

"Yes."

The "yes" was enough for me to follow him out of the Underground and return to street level. Quentin carefully closed the door, setting the lock back in place. Cautiously, he scanned the alley before guiding us across the cobblestones and back onto public streets. My knee ached with every step, but was functional.

We zig-zagged our way to a four-way intersection. Across the street was the iron pergola, its shimmering glass canopy a beacon. A sign that the ferry was near. Home just beyond that.

Quentin reached for my hand and pulled me toward the street, the walk signal flashing an obvious red across the street. And they hit. Tingles. Like a freight train with-

out warning, knocking me to the ground. The fire. The shadow. The shower of painful rain.

A ring of fire.

A shadow reaching and drawing back. Reaching and drawing back.

Rain. Piercing. Painful.

I was tired. I wanted it to be done.

"Show me," I yelled. "Show me your face."

And what had been abstract moments before, turned real. Too real. Revealing Quentin's face, his arm, reaching in and out of the singing fire. Reaching for me. Trying to pull me out.

I screamed.

"CeeCee!"

I couldn't stop screaming. In my head. Outside of my head.

"CeeCee! Open your eyes!" He had scooped me up. I knew we were moving. Crossing the street to the pergola on the other side.

The fire turned dark, fading Quentin's attempt at liberating me from the flames. I clung to his neck, scared of what I saw. I couldn't let go, scared of what it meant.

My body bounced in his arms, my screams subsided. I knew the consequence of asking to see the vision. I knew if I opened my eyes I would see nothing. Nothing until Quentin released me from the darkness.

A cool line slithered slowly across the back of my neck,

sending a river of chills down my spine. I reached up, but all I felt was the ice of my own fingers touching my skin.

"CeeCee, open your eyes and look at me!"

We stopped. He set me down, the cold cement immediately seeped through my coat. "Quentin! The fire, it was you reaching into the fire."

"I don't care. Open your eyes and look at me!"

"I can't. I can't see."

"Open your eyes and look at me!" he commanded. Expecting. Waiting.

Nothing. I opened my eyes and nothing.

Close. Open. Nothing.

It didn't work.

Only darkness remained. A strange calm whispered from my mouth. "It didn't work. I can't see."

"It has to work. They said it would work. Open your eyes and look at me! Open your eyes and look at me! Open your eyes and look at me!" he urgently repeated in quick succession.

"It's not working."

"Damn it! Open your eyes! Look at me!"

"Quentin . . ."

"OPEN. YOUR. EYES!" I could hear the exhaustion, the panic, the loss of control welling up in his voice. "LOOK AT . . . me."

I wished, in that moment, for the strength of my mother to come back. I slipped my hand in my coat to touch

her pearls, her wisdom. My hand rubbed my chest. Up. Down. Nothing. To my sides. Again, nothing. They were gone. The slithering across my neck now making sense.

I tried to sit up, move my feet underneath me. "Quentin. My mother's pearls. They fell off. They can't be far. I can't lose them. Her."

"What are you doing? You can't see!"

"Her pearls. The slipped off. Not far. Across the road. Pleeeease," I pleaded. "I can't lose another part of her."

"FUCK!" he roared in frustration. "Don't move!"

I sat. Blind to everything. My hands planted firmly on the cold ground, sending wave after wave of chills through me. The sounds I thought were nothing began to grow all around me. My heightened sense sharpening the small pieces of noise tunneling into my ears. Somewhere ahead of me, I heard the revving of a diesel engine sputter to life up the hill. It groaned. The squeal of metal stretching in forward movement.

And then a SNAP! So loud and foreign, it raised every hair on my body to attention.

A symphony of uproar kicked in, overwhelming my ears. Cars were honking. Breaks were squealing. The few people still milling around began to scream. I sat helpless, with no idea where danger lurked.

"Quentin!" my voice screeched out.

I tried to place the noise — the spinning whine of an engine set in motion but not started. The screams grew,

gears grinding against themselves. "Get her out of there!"

Get who out of where? "QUENTIN!"

"CEECEE!" I heard him. Faintly. Above the chaos. The only picture in my head was of him reaching into the flames. Trying to get to me.

But it all came to a screeching halt.

Silence.

Nothing. But. Silence.

For one.

Single.

Breath.

Until metal ground against the iron pergola, consuming me in an ear-splitting explosion. I was thrown back and the crackling of fire heated my once cold skin. And soon it began to rain. Shards of tiny glass rained down, piercing my bare legs.

I curled up.

I focused on my mom's face.

And I waited.

I was not afraid to die.

CHAPTER
44

I hovered in darkness, circling with Quentin in a pool of silver light. There was no noise. No nothing. Just us. Together. Dancing our silent dance. On and on we spun, Quentin's shadow reaching out, and pounding back the threatening danger.

It was peaceful.

Beautiful.

The moment deliriously euphoric.

Pools of deep emeralds twinkled down at me.

Here I was happy to remain.

Forever.

With him.

"Cee," he whispered in my ear. "Please."

It was his "please" that caused my foot to falter. It was sad. Inconsolable. I touched his cheek, reassuring him.

"Please. Look at me," he said again, his eyes of pleasure not matching the sorrow in his voice. "You have to open your eyes."

But they were open, I wanted to say. Forever open. Drinking in the brightness.

"Please, CeeCee." Rawness rattled from his throat, pulling his shadow tight around us. "Open your eyes."

The encroaching darkness was persistent. Pushing in. Battling against our small pool of light. Quentin's shadow was no match for the eternity of darkness that waited patiently for us to step into.

He mumbled something I couldn't hear. I leaned closer. A whooshing pulse rattled loud in my ear.

He spoke again.

I watched as his lips moved, but the sound was muddled, unformed.

Another voice joined in, projecting through the darkness. And another. And another. I could no longer distinguish Quentin's from the rest. They morphed, they blended, bending time and space.

My arms tightened around him. Squeezing.

Refusing to let go.

Clinging tight to nothing.

Nothing but a shadow.

CHAPTER

45

Beep.

Beep. Whoosh.

Beep.

They were constant, invading every crevice inside of me.

Beep. Whoosh.

I couldn't place them.

Beep.

I crested up from the dusky shadows, landing in the SAM, every square inch of the room filled with Picasso. One on top of the other. Not a sliver of wall to be seen.

"I am her grandmother. You will let me in."

Beep. Whoosh. Beep.

I spun. Looking for the voice. Looking for Evelyn.

"I'm sorry ma'am. Your name does not appear on the guest list. If you could please wait until her father returns, we can speak with him."

Beep.

She was here. On the other side of the barrier. I waved. Frantically. She couldn't see me.

"I'll. Wait."

All was quiet again, except for the beeps.

And a whoosh.

Beep. Beep. The high-pitched frequency irritated my senses.

Beep. Whoosh.

Beep.

The shadows morphed into a dark forest and I stepped in. Trees. Everywhere. My body bent in unison with their sway. Languishing in their simple strength.

"The ticket will be waiting for you at the airport. Your flight leaves at two."

Dad? His voice floated by, bounced from limb to limb, and then burst as it flew away. Wait! Where are you going?

Beep.

Time floated on wings, passed through the shadows, pouring into a vat of nothingness.

Beep.

Beep.

Woosh.

CHAPTER
46

I opened my eyes, but saw nothing.

Pain gnawed at every ounce of my being.

I closed them. Opened them.

Gray. A warm, fuzzy gray painted over everything.

It was a little bit yellow.

A little bit red.

A little bit black.

A little bit of nothing.

"Hello?" I hardly recognized the whisper that gurgled up from my own throat.

"CeeCee?" His voice was groggy. Beautiful. Refreshing.

I turned my head to him. Nauseousness rose to the back of my mouth, my eyes unseeing. "Quentin? Where are we?"

"The hospital." I felt a hand slide and wrap gently around my own. Warm. Strong.

I swallowed and closed my eyes. I didn't need them. "How long . . ?"

"Two days."

"I can't see."

"I know. I'm sorry." His voice cracked. I wanted to reach out and assure him, but I didn't know how to lift my fingers to find his face. "I've tried . . ."

"Where's Dad?"

"He stepped out to stretch his legs. I'll go get him."

"NO!" I held tight to his hand, trying to lift my other one, but it was weighted down, impossible to lift. "Don't leave me. Please."

"I'm here."

"I can't lift my arm."

"It's in a cast."

"What happened?"

The gentle whisper of his fingertips trailed a caress across my cheek. "It all happened so fast, Cee. I couldn't get to you. I tried. The flames were everywhere. I thought you . . ." His eyes saw what mine couldn't. An agony he alone would bear.

"Tell me what happened."

"Let me get your Dad."

I squeezed his hand hard, holding tight to the lifeline outside of me. "Please, Quentin. Tell me what happened.

The last thing I remember was you carrying me across the street to the pergola."

"There was an industrial tow truck up the street from us. It was pulling a large dump truck. The cables snapped and the truck came barreling down the street backward, taking two cars . . ."

"CeeCee! Are you awake?" I could hear Dad's cane lancing off things left and right, the sound moving closer, his eyes unable to see my unseeing eyes.

Like father, like daughter.

"Peter," I heard Quentin say quietly as he left my hand cold and empty. "Here. Come around this side."

There was a shuffle. The bed bent under a new weight. A rough hand filled the emptiness Quentin had left in mine. Dad pressed his lips tight against my knuckles. "Thank God. We weren't sure. You were unconscious for so long. And the burns. Oh, thank God."

"What burns?"

There was silence. Except for the beep.

And the whoosh.

Beep.

Whoosh.

"What burns? Will someone please talk to me? Dad? Quentin?" The beeps grew faster. Followed by a quick exhaling whoosh. Faster and faster, keeping tempo with my apprehension.

It was Dad who finally said, "Maybe we should let the nurse know you're awake."

ART IS THE LIE

"Tell me!" My voice jarring even me.

"It's your legs, Cee." I could hear the hesitancy in his words. He squeezed my hand harder and said, "The fire moved quickly before Quentin was able to get around the other side and pull you out."

"Pull me out?" I asked in horror. I tried to move them, but I couldn't feel them. It was as if they didn't exist. "I can't feel them."

"That's because they have you on pain medicine. The doctor assures us the burns will heal with time. They shouldn't be part of any ongoing problems."

Unlike my eyes. "Dad, I can't see. Why wasn't Quentin able to restore my sight?"

His thumb ran roughly back and forth on the tops of my knuckles. His delay sent dread into the lowest part of me. Finally, he said, "I don't know."

"You have to call her, Dad. You have to call Evelyn and find out why it didn't work."

The silence could be heard a mile away. "Maybe we should let the nurse know you are awake."

He didn't need to bother. The symphony of beeps and whooshes brought her to us.

"Is everything all right in here?" a sweet, southern voice called out.

Dad squeezed my hand. "She's awake."

"Claire Claire Vanderbie," the voice chimed a full name nobody used. "We're glad to see you. You've had two gentlemen very concerned about you."

CHAPTER
47

"You couldn't live without me, could you?"

Foster had arrived the next day in Foster fashion, teasing me after he was assured I was somewhat sane. "You didn't need to go to such extremes to get me home from school. Although, I appreciate the out on the Trig test I got to reschedule for next week."

"You didn't have to come home."

"Yes, I did. Otherwise, who would protect you from the chaos about to burst through your door."

"What chaos?"

And chaos it was. Aunt Lucy, Uncle Russell, and the twins came barreling through. I could feel their bodies cramming into the small room, turning the air warm. The noise rattled my only good sense.

"I'll wait outside," Quentin breathed in my ear.

"Oh, no," I whispered back. "You cannot leave me alone with these people."

"These people are your people."

"Please. Stay." His hand slipped back into mine.

My dad's voice emerged above the rumpus. "Lucy. Russell. We're limiting visits, so Cee . . ."

"Oh my god. Oh my god. Oh my god." It was Summer. It was drama I was not prepared for. "I told myself I wouldn't cry, but CeeCee. Oh my god. Your poor little body. Your face." She broke down crying, confirming that Dad and Quentin had been overly kind in their assessments of my injuries. I was at least thankful she didn't throw her body across mine.

"Summer, please," Aunt Lucy piped in, her skirt swishing its way to the bed. "CeeCee, we were devastated to hear about the accident."

I doubt it. "Thanks."

Her long fingers touched my shoulder. "This is so unfortunate. Everything. The accident. Your eyes."

I squeezed Quentin's fingers tight, hoping the reminder of him standing next to me would help me to keep my mouth shut. "I'm sure we'll figure it out."

"Of course you will." She was patronizing me.

"This looks to be a Vanderbie family reunion."

A rush of air swirled over me and froze as my aunt spun toward the new voice, everything cementing to stillness. Nothing moved except the sound waves carrying Eveyln's voice to my ears.

"Mother." Lucy's voice took on a new edge. I heard her move back through the room. "You shouldn't be here."

"I was invited."

"By whom?"

"By me." Dad. He'd called her.

"You invited Mother? Here?" Shock rattled her cool demeanor. "Since when are you two talking?"

"Since it seems we have family business to take care of." The strength in her voice left no room for questioning. "Russell, if you and the girls wouldn't mind waiting in the hall, I need to speak with my children."

"What about him?" Summer whined.

"Quentin stays," Evelyn replied empathically.

The dust settled around us and Dad spoke up, introducing Evelyn to Foster. "Mom, this is my son, Foster."

"Foster. Finally, we meet. I've been getting updates on you for quite some time, but it is nice to finally see you in person. I hope we have another opportunity that is not filled with such unpleasant circumstances to get to know each other."

"Um, it's nice to meet you, too." Oh, Foster. I could hear the broken confusion in his tone.

In her no nonsense way, she got right to business, dispensing with all pleasantries. "Well, it seems we have two visionaries in the family, but you already knew that, didn't you Lucy?"

Aunt Lucy began to sputter. "I don't know what . . ."

"I think you do know what I'm talking about, and you made a conscious choice to do nothing about it." Evelyn stood next to me, her sweet scent wafting around my bed. The bed bent and a set of cold fingers touched down on my eyebrows, startling me. They walked slowly, from one side of my face to the other, touching what I could not see. Evelyn's fingers continued their soft parade around my face, but it was Lucy she directed her steel voice to. "Lucia, my hopes were pinned high when you were born on the day celebrating the Patron Saint Lucia."

"The story is old mother. You've told us before," the belittling tone mocking her namesake. "St. Lucy. The saint of light. Bringing light to those lost in the dark. But you bestowed the name on the wrong person."

Her fingers abruptly left my face as she stood, her disappointment cutting through her tone. "My hopes were never for you to have the visions. That is a curse all its own. My hope was always for you to extend generosity and benevolence on those in need. But when someone was in the greatest of need, you failed to help. Not only failed, but made a calculating choice to leave him locked in the dark indefinitely."

"It's always been about him," she seethed. "Even now, after years of snubbing you, our family, our gift, here you are, with arms wide open, welcoming your prodigal son home."

"Um, excuse me." It was Foster, confusion ringing loud and clear. I felt awful, wishing I could lessen the punch, but there was nothing I could do at this point. I had no idea where this conversation was going. "What are you two talking about?"

"I'm sorry Foster," Evelyn replied. "I realize this is quite a shock and will take some time to fully understand. But if you could please grant us a little patience as we hash through the details, I think all will become clear."

Her voice turned back to me. "CeeCee, I'm sure it was quite disconcerting when Quentin was unable to release you from the darkness, but I am guessing the vision you chose to see was about him. Am I correct?"

"Yes."

"Guardians are unable to draw you out when the vision has been about them. You need a restorer."

"A what?" Half the room said in unison. Only Lucy's voice remained quiet.

"Our gifts are based on a triad. A balance of powers. It has been this way through the generations. A visionary is born with the gift. The gift is released when a guardian is introduced. And the restorer, weaving between the visionary and guardian, balance out the powers. Protecting them both."

"How do we find my restorer?" I asked.

"Well, he's here," she said like it was the most obvious thing. "Standing next to you."

I knew Quentin was on one side of me, so that left Foster. "Foster? Foster's my restorer?"

"Yes. A visionary's restorer is always their sibling."

"What if I didn't have a sibling?"

"Than the gift would never have released."

"WHAT are you people *talking* about?" Poor Foster.

"Foster, would you please indulge me for a moment."

"No . . . um, I don't know . . ." Hesitation drew out his words.

"Please, Foster," she coaxed, "I need you to sit down next to your sister."

I didn't hear any movement, my heart was racing.

After what felt like an eternity, the bed bent under Foster's weight.

"Perfect," Evelyn chimed. "Now, Quentin, please help CeeCee to sit forward so Foster can get his arm around her shoulder."

Quentin gently placed his hands on the back of my shoulders and pulled me forward off my pillow. I waited to feel Foster's arm around me, but there was no movement from where he sat on the bed.

"Foster, I need you to place your hands over your sister's eyes, and repeat after me." I could hear the impatience in Evelyn's voice.

Foster didn't move.

"Please, Foster," I whispered. "I promise to explain everything."

"I swear, CeeCee," his strained voice volleyed back. "If this is some practical joke you are recording, I will never . . ."

It was Dad who finally said, "Foster, please. I assure you, this is no joke."

The weight on the bed shifted, and I felt Foster's arm go around the back of my shoulders before his warm hands softly covered over my eyes.

"Now, please," Evelyn continued, "repeat after me: Upon swift wings, let this curse take flight."

His voice was horse, hesitant. "Upon swift wings, um . . . let this curse take flight."

"Strip away the night and with my voice restore light."

"Strip away the . . ."

"Strip away the night and with my voice restore light," she repeated.

"Strip away the night and with my voice restore light."

The gray erupted behind Foster's hands. It poured into blue, into yellow, into red. The colors took flight and tangoed together. Twisting. The palette exploding as Foster dropped his hands from my eyes.

Slowly. Like the birth of a new day. I opened my eyes to

beautiful,

alluring,

crystal greens staring back at me.

EPILOGUE

"Claire Claire?" Quentin asked as his thumb drew lazy circles around my knuckles. Unable to stand being cooped up in the house any longer, he'd carried me up to my sanctuary where we lounged on the couch, my burnt legs propped over his. All was quiet. Normal. For now. "Is your name really Claire Claire?"

It had been three weeks since the accident. Twenty-one days since Foster had restored my sight and Aunt Lucy groveled for forgiveness after she released Dad from his long endured blindness. A darkness he'd become trapped in after granting a vision about my mom. The first and only vision he'd granted, causing their car to spin out of control.

"My parents thought too much alike." I tried to explain the secret ballot scheme they'd hatched before I was

born, sealing their favorite names into envelopes. "After I popped out, they ripped open their exchanged envelopes like a couple of giddy school girls and realized they'd chosen the exact same name. So, in a moment of brilliance, they gave me both."

He lifted my hand to his lips and trailed a line of kisses up my arm. "You were a moment of brilliance."

I pulled my arm from his grip, embarrassed by the compliment. "Now you're just brown-nosing me, because you want your Christmas gift." I reached over the back of the couch and pulled out a canvas wrapped in brown paper and handed it to him.

"When, exactly, did you get out and shop?" he teased, knowing full well I hadn't left the house since the accident.

Everyone had come to visit at first. Their words of concern emphasizing how lucky I was to have survived such an ordeal. But none saw under the bandages on my legs. Not even the green-eyed boy sitting next to me. He was the only person that still came almost every day. Sometimes we would talk or watch a movie, but mostly we sat in silence as I selfishly held onto the illusion that he would still be here once the bandages came off.

I shrugged. "Just open it." I didn't know how long my nerves would hold out before I snatched it back.

He lifted the paper off and turned the canvas over, exposing a wash of reds and silver, my own words embedded between swirls of thread and wire:

I thought to be brave,
I had to not be afraid.
But in truth,
it is about being terrified
and forging forward anyway.

The clock ticked loudly in the endless silence, while his eyes roamed across the canvas. I hadn't realized I'd been holding my breath until Quentin quietly said, "CeeCee, this is beautiful." He looked up and snaked his hand around the back of my head, drawing me to him. "Truthful." His lips fastened tight on top of mine.

He released his hold on my head and said, "I have something for you."

He leaned the canvas against the couch and reached in his pocket, pulling out a small black box topped with a perfect silver bow.

"You didn't have to get me anything."

"I didn't," he answered slyly.

I quickly pulled off the bow and lifted the lid, gently pulling back the folds of tissue. My breath caught. My heart raced. The past bounced beautifully back into my future. The pearls I thought lost forever, peaked out from where they were safely nestled on the tissue.

I bit my lip to hold back the water works that threatened to unleash. "I thought it had been destroyed . . ."

"No, it was in my pocket." He took the necklace from me and pulled it over my head. "The clasp was broken, but not anymore."

My hands wrapped around the sides of his face as I scooted closer. "Who are you? Where did you come from?"

"Your imagination, I suspect," he answered with a grin. A beautiful, raw, heart-melting grin.

"My thoughts exactly."

THE END

ACKNOWLEDGEMENTS

Honestly, I don't know where to begin, because if it takes a village to raise a family, an entire city is needed to write a book!

First, I would like to thank my muse, my confidant, my best friend, my sister, Carrie Cook Minns (carrieminns.com), who's writing talents are the benchmark I strive for. To my late mom, dad and brother, Tim, who have unconditionally supported me in all of my many creative and crazy endeavors.

To the ever-amazing Linda Anderson, my writing and critique partner — what would I have ever gotten done without our weekly check-ins? And to the wise and wonderful Peggy King Anderson. I could not have asked for a better coach and cheerleader.

To Linda Keeney and Tegan Tigani for championing me and continually reminding me that it just takes one brave thing a day.

To Ken Grant at MotivatedBranding for giving me the swift kick I needed to climb over my hurdles. It's all about the boots, right?

To Christy Watson for red penning not one, but three full manuscripts.

To Myra Waddel, Erika Fox, Tami Kays, Lisa Aldofson, and Alison Shane for taking fresh reads and giving me in-

sightful feedback. To Michelle Perkins for margaritas on the front lawn, because what is better than that?

To my posse of moms: Alison, Tami, Trish, Rocio, Jenni, Jamie, Iveth, Suzann — you are my sanity.

To Katy Tuttle and her ever amazing talents of making me look good.

To all of the readers who rolled the dice, took a chance on me, and gave me the thumbs up.

And last, but most definitely not least, my guys — Patrick, Rylan, and Kincaid. How did I ever get so lucky? xoxo

ABOUT THE AUTHOR

I dream. I spin. I create. I write.

And somewhere, from the dark corners of my mind, shadows emerge, slipping in and out of my conscious. They move closer, come to life, and grow, until my imaginary friends are as real to me as anyone I've known my entire life. It is then I sit and begin to type.

I type with a spirit for the young at heart — the ones who set the tone of my characters and reveal their direction, their nuances, their meaning. It is a privilege and a gift that continually awes and inspires me.

I studied art at the University of Oregon and am a member of the Western Washington chapter of SCBWI International.

When I'm not behind my computer typing, writing and developing my stories, I can be found flitting around the beautiful, creative island and hub I call home, a stone's throw from Seattle, Washington, with my husband, two boys, and one nutty dog.

Cheers!

www.courtneyhopp.com

ART IS THE LIE